TO K[

Colby had finally decided on a way. It was simple and yet it was also perfect. In the telling, it would not be much. But in the performance it would be great indeed.

He went to the window of the room in which Mullin was sitting. The sheriff had left him. The old man sat with his face in his hands. How great the convulsion of his soul must have been, when it made his very body shake. The fingers quivered. The white hair shook. But Colby had no pity for white hair. His own would soon be silver.

Slowly, with infinite care, he raised the window. It didn't make a sound. But though the noise didn't alarm the watchman, those keen eyes looking in upon him from the night would do so.

With indescribable relish Colby saw the hands fall from the face of Mullin, saw him raise his head, saw him begin to turn his head by slow degrees. There was a nightmare of terror in the soul of old Mullin. It brought shining drops of perspiration to his forehead. But at length his head was moved far enough for him to make out that the window was indeed open.

He leaped to his feet with a shriek. And there, in the window, he was confronting Harrison Colby, and the outlaw was smiling in the intensity of his enjoyment.

Fear would have struck the old man to the floor. But Colby did not wait for that.

"A present from Colby, sheriff," he shouted through the house, and raised his gun....

Other *Leisure* Westerns by Max Brand:
KING CHARLIE
RED DEVIL OF THE RANGE
PRIDE OF TYSON
THE OUTLAW TAMER
BULL HUNTER'S ROMANCE
BULL HUNTER
TIGER MAN
GUN GENTLEMEN
THE MUSTANG HERDER
WESTERN TOMMY
SPEEDY
THE WHITE WOLF
TROUBLE IN TIMBERLINE
TIMBAL GULCH TRAIL
THE BELLS OF SAN FILIPO
MARBLEFACE
THE RETURN OF THE RANCHER
RONICKY DOONE'S REWARD
RONICKY DOONE'S TREASURE
RONICKY DOONE
THE WHISPERING OUTLAW
THE SHADOW OF SILVER TIP
THE TRAP AT COMANCHE BEND
THE MOUNTAIN FUGITIVE

MAX BRAND

WOODEN GUNS

LEISURE BOOKS   NEW YORK CITY

A LEISURE BOOK®

April 1997

Published by special arrangement with Golden West
Literary Agency.

Dorchester Publishing Co., Inc.
276 Fifth Avenue
New York, NY 10001

Printed in the United States of America.

CHAPTER ONE

OVERCOMING A HANDICAP

All the upper forest was alive. The aspens by the watercourse lashed back and forth; the great pines bowed gravely to one another; but beneath the treetops there was a level of greater quiet, for it was a wood of unusual size and unusual density. The ax of the lumberman had not thinned it. Perhaps the reason was that it was so inaccessible, for the mountains sloped on either side down to burning deserts.

One could stand on a hill shoulder and glance to bare summits on the one side, where patches of snow still lay in the northern shadow of the big rocks above timber line; and on the other hand one's eye fell to the wide and yellow sands of the desert over which clouds rarely passed. The storm winds condensed their mists only about the summits of the range. From those peaks the clouds would blow out like stiffly standing flags, snapping away to nothing at the ends, and only on the sides of the mountains fell the snow above timber line and the rains beneath it.

1

The very watercourses had not the courage to face the naked country, so it seemed, for shortly after they left their ravines among the hills, their valleys flattened out and the streams themselves sank into the sands or were drunk up by the fierce sun.

But midway down the mountains the forest was a royal one, and since there were no great waterways down which to float the logs, and since cartage across the desert was almost impossible, the wood choppers had not yet thinned the ranks of the giants.

In the midst of this sheltered region, where a fault curved over the throat of a mountain, a slit of rocks across the forest, a mine stood. Here, as the bared rocks dipped into the woods again, they had sunk their shaft, breaking the ground with infinite labor, for it was steel-hard quartzite. It paid just a little under the cost of driving the hole, for it was such a vein as leads men on and on, here thick and promising to grow thicker, and again pinching out to a miserable color and no more.

They had been laboring for two months now, and Conover, as he stepped back to view the darkening gap of the shaft, wondered if they might not have to work for two years before they got to the heart of the vein.

Then he turned back to the fire. The coffee was prepared, and the pone had been stirred up for some time; but still there was no meat, and there would be none unless Buck had found luck in his hunting. Since they had already hunted over the surrounding district thoroughly, the meat problem had been growing in difficulty. So Conover eyed the dark mass of the woods and listened to the roar of the storm with increasing anxiety.

He was a big man, from his great, corded neck to his heavily booted feet. He must have been an inch or two over six feet, and yet his width of shoulders and his length of arm made him seem hardly more than the average. He was made for action, and action had been his. Even the flannel shirt could not quite mask the ripple of the muscles down his arms and across his back, and in his face there were seams and marks of weariness and labor. He could not have been more than thirty, but he looked much more, as if he had lived enough to crowd a full lifetime with events.

As he stood there, indeed, he was the warrior type. Had he been born five hundred years before he would have been clad in armor with a famous sword buckled at his side and a famous title after his name. But since he lived in the twentieth century, he was here on the western frontier with only these rocks to use his strength upon, and only drill and double jack for weapons.

He was born in the wrong time to attain the greatest things, and yet there was about him that atmosphere of power which does not lie in the muscles alone, but which is of the spirit also.

The moment he moved to pick up some wood to freshen the fire, however, it was apparent that all was not well with this magnificent machine.

A step as light as the step of a boy might be expected, for the restless and piercing eye of Conover showed nerve power as sharply concentrated and strong as his big muscles. But now that he stirred, his right foot trailed in an odd fashion. One could not say exactly what was wrong. It was not the limp of a man who has pulled a tendon or bruised his flesh, but it was rather like the walk of a man whose weight had rested on one leg for a long time and put the limb asleep for lack of blood.

Now, as he leaned, there was the same baffling uncertainty discernible about the right hand. In fact, he changed his mind at the last moment and picked up the wood with his left hand instead of the right which he had at first advanced.

After he had thrown it on the fire he remained for a moment staring down to that great right hand. Then, with a sigh, he turned his back on the fire to let it burn as it might

4

and went into the little lean-to which he and Buck had thrown up against the side of a boulder. There he sat down at an improvised table and lighted a pine torch.

Before him he set up a little square mirror. He took a paper and pencil and began to work with the utmost labor, drawing out his letters as large, as sprawling, and as ragged as those which a five-year-old child makes when with undisciplined nerves and muscles it attempts to copy the sample of writing before it. Conover used his left hand; moreover, he did not look down at the paper, but kept his eyes fixed steadily in the mirror.

It made a task easy in the telling, but strangely difficult in the performance, for the image of the letters which he formed was inverted, of course, and his clumsy left hand was compelled to do the opposite of what the eye told the muscles. It was, in short, that system of training by which left-handed people are taught to use their right hands. And here it came bitterly hard to Conover. For it was only during the last year that his right hand had ceased to be his most effective tool.

The tragedy had occurred a year before. The shot which had not exploded for half an hour after the rest of the round, had burst as he was advancing upon the place. Some premonition had made him swerve at the last instant, and therefore the full effect of the shock had come upon his right side.

Buck had dragged his battered companion out of the gap, and then he had carted him out of the mountains to the first doctor.

But that was only the beginning. For six months the most optimistic opinion had been that the right leg and the right arm would be paralyzed forever. Then life began to appear in them suddenly. The shattered nerves began to function slowly, responding in some degree to the impulses which the brain was sending down. Finally he could walk without a crutch; then he could lift and carry. But still the hand was so clumsy that he could not cut his own meat.

It could hold a drill, however, and the left hand was taught to wield a single jack. So Conover went out again on a trail prospecting, and, in company with Buck, his old companion, steered his way into the mountains, sighting a course between the long ears of a burro.

Every day he worked at the system which the doctor had planned for him. Every spare hour was put into the labor of giving that left hand the adroitness which his right hand had once possessed.

"And try the right hand, too, now and then," the doctor had said. "God knows what's wrong with that right side of yours; it's as healthy as the left. The nerves have had a battering, of course, but the chief trouble is in your mind, Conover. You've been doubting that right hand of yours for so long that you can't see it for yourself functioning as it used to do. Give it a chance and then see. Good-by, and keep hoping!"

Conover had never forgotten. And once a day, religiously, he made the effort. Once a day he stopped the work with the left hand and attempted to write with the other. And to-day, this was the time he chose, while he labored in the shack in agony of spirit, waiting for the return of Buck.

He laid down the pencil, and he closed his eyes. Centering all the might of his will until his clenched jaws ached and his whole body trembled, he vowed that this time he would succeed; this time, certainly, he would so focus his attention that the doctor himself would be satisfied.

Then he opened his eyes, scooped up the pencil in his right hand, and laid the point of it upon the paper. "Jim Conover," he started to write. Alas! The first line was a jagged dip to the left. The next was a wild swoop which carried the pencil's point entirely off the paper.

Conover sank back with a groan. It was death to him. It was worse than death, for death comes only once, and this torment came every day of his life.

He looked up to see that Buck was standing before him, and across his shoulders was the body of a deer; for his hunt that day had been a lucky one. Yet there was no happiness in his glance. He met the miserable eyes of Conover with a moisture of pity and sympathy in his own.

They said not a word. The mirror, the pencil, and the paper were all laid to the side, and Conover went out to brighten the fire, while Buck cut the venison into collops to be roasted on splinters of wood over the blaze. The pone, too, was cooked, and the coffee brought to the boiling point, when its fragrance swept pleasantly to the nostrils of the two hungry men.

It was pitch dark when they began to eat, with Conover listening while Buck gave all the details of his hunt. He was one of those men who put in every detail. He could relate how he laced his shoes at such length that it would wear out an entire meal.

There had been nothing of interest in his shooting of the deer this evening, but he dragged it out until Conover had covered every step of the trail with him.

He was the exact opposite of Conover, for he was a scant, withered fragment of a man, fifty years old and white as three-score and ten, with a pair of wild, blue eyes flashing in his face.

"And so you downed him?" said Conover toward the close, when he had finished his second cup of coffee.

But it was foolish to attempt to shorten one of Buck's narratives. He picked it up exactly where the blunt bass voice of Conover had broken into the tale.

"It was getting dusk, as I was saying," he went on. "Looked like smoke was floating around under the trees—black smoke, Conover, like some kinds of powder gives off. Speaking of powder I remember when——"

"Let's have the powder later on," said Conover patiently. "I want to know how you killed that deer."

"I'm telling you. It was getting dark fast, and that deer's head didn't look no clearer than a face you see in a fog. It was plumb dim. So I says to myself: 'Buck,' says I, 'the best thing would be to walk around the side of that bush that's standing in between you and the deer and get a look at its whole body. Or else you'll be shooting at a ghost, and dead ghosts don't fill no bellies as big as Jim Conover's.'"

"Thanks," said Conover dryly, "for thinking about me."

"But I seen," said Buck, "that if I walked around the bush the darned deer might hear me or see me, and then I'd have nothing but a streak among the shadows to shoot at. So I looked around for the best thing to help me get my bead—"

"That sure was a dog-gone patient deer," observed Conover at this point.

"How can I get on with you talking all the time?" said the little man, shrugging his shoulders and frowning in anger. "Darned if I ain't got a mind not to finish the story."

"No, no!" put in Conover with an eager penitence. "I'm plumb interested, Buck."

"Well," said Buck, "I seen a scalped place on a bough that was hanging low down right near the head of the deer. I says to myself that I'll hold a bead on that gray-looking place until I got dead centered, and then I'll hop off that mark and take a bang at the head of the meat we needed.

"So I got down on one knee and never took my eyes off the mark, but just felt beneath me to make sure that that knee wasn't coming down on any twig or nothing that would crackle. When I had myself kneeling and the gun leveled I says to myself that the worst part of the job was over. So I begun to settle myself to get comfortable——"

He stopped talking and glared at Conover. But the vacant eye of the latter took no notice of the fact that the voice of his friend had ceased flowing. Plainly he was contemplating his own thoughts, and a bright spot of red jumped into the center of the little man's cheek.

"Well," he said, "I guess we might clean up the dishes."

"Pretty near time," agreed Conover, and they began to work, both in silence, until finally the big man started. "Buck," he said, "seems to me that you didn't finish telling me about how you shot that deer."

"I seen you wasn't listening," said Buck sadly. "I guess you get plumb tired of me, Conover."

Jim Conover laid a big hand upon the shoulder of his friend.

"Partner," he said, "I'm mighty sorry. But I had some news to-day. Couldn't keep it out of my head even while you was talking."

"What's up?" said Buck gloomily, suspicious of an invented excuse.

"The Marvin kid rode up with the mail. There wasn't nothing for you, but dog-goned if he didn't have a letter for me."

He took it from his pocket and extended it to Buck: "Take a look for yourself."

CHAPTER TWO

UPSETTING NEWS

It was a stained envelope, all of the dirt upon which could hardly have come during its passage through the mails. Perhaps some had come in the pocket of the Marvin boy; perhaps some had come in the pocket of Conover. But there were other marks which could only have been made by the hand of the writer.

There was a round, semitransparent place suspiciously like that which a drop of melted butter would have left, and there was, moreover, a great smudge of ink sweeping away from the address with the print of the guilty man stamped plainly on the paper.

From the envelope Buck extracted a single folded sheet of paper, ruled, and written on both sides in a clumsy hand which seemed to have the unformed nature of a child's writing as well as the tremulous uncertainty of age. It read:

DEAR JIMMY: We have been waiting all these years to hear from you and to see you ag'in. Now we've spotted you I guess it will be too late for me. I'm lying in bed with my last sickness, Doc Anderson says. And the doc is a darned smart man, as you know. Maybe by riding fast and hard you could get down here to say good-by to me, and it would sure comfort me a lot to have a look at you before I step out through the door.

Maybe you got some important business that you can't leave. If you have, I ain't going to bother you to come. But if you ain't, come along, son, and lemme have a last look at you.

About the way that folks would treat you down around here, you don't need to have no worries. They've forgot a lot. And the rest they lay up agin' the fact that you was just a wild young kid.

Well, son, if I don't see you ag'in, God bless you and keep care of you and forgive me for not giving you a better rearing up!   DAD.

When the eyes of Buck, alert enough at all other matters but singularly slow and dull in dealing with letters, trailed down through the last sentence and reached the signature, he gasped with astonishment, refolded the letter, and then opened it again. He read every word once more before he replaced the letter in the envelope and handed it back to his companion.

Great stress of emotion for once made Buck almost terse in his speech.

"Partner," he said, packing a load of tobacco into his pipe and stabbing it viciously home with his forefinger, "you've had this here bad news on your mind all this time and yet you been letting me ramble along about nothing? Reminds me of what—but tell me what you going to do, Jim?"

"I got to go, Buck."

The latter sighed. "Dog-gone me," he said, "if I didn't know that there was trouble ahead, and I smelled something wrong when I seen that envelope. It had a look to me like a man with a bad face. Well, Jim, how long will it take you to get there?"

"About two weeks, riding."

"Two weeks! And then another week down there and two weeks more coming back. Why, son, it'll be five weeks before I lay eyes on you ag'in."

Conover nodded. "I'll make over my share of this here mine to you, Buck," he said. "The Marvin kid said that his brother would like to take a hand in here. He's got an idea that there's gold down in these here rocks. Marvin could go in with you, and—"

"The devil!" said Buck.

He said no more, but Conover did not re-open the suggestion of a new partner at the mine.

"Where's your home country?" asked Buck at last.

Conover smiled: "How long have I knowed you, Buck?"

"Coming on to three years, old-timer, and darn long years, at that, packed full of action!"

"Have I ever told you about my home country?"

"Can't say that you have."

"Then I guess you can figure that there's a reason why."

"There must be a reason, Jim."

"There is, too."

"Guns?"

"Yep, guns."

"Dog-goned if that ain't a shame."

"Nope, it's the best thing that could of happened to me."

"Are you wearing a made-up name, Jim?"

"I'm wearing my right name, but—suppose I was to tell you the whole story, Buck? It's owing to you, anyway?"

"I'll tell a man that I'd be tickled to know."

The big man hesitated, as though at a loss for a place where he could begin. Then he whistled, and a horse ran out of the blackness of the forest and came within the outer ring of the firelight. There he remained, shaking his head up and down, his great eyes bright with mischief and the desire to steal away, though the call of his master held him.

"Look there," said Jim, and at the sound of the familiar voice the big horse came a tentative step closer.

"He's a whale of a hoss," said Buck admiringly. "Dog-gone me if I wouldn't give my eyeteeth just for the sake of riding that devil for five minutes. But I'd rather face five guns than five minutes on his back. He'd eat me up."

"Well," said Jim Conover, "that's the way I was when I was a kid. There wasn't nobody that could ride me, and I was sure aching for a fight all the time. Me being big and sort of hard looking, it wasn't everybody that would take me on for a fight. But I'd wait until a chance come along for me to jump two men at once.

"Nacherally, fighting with the fists led into fighting with knives and guns. Gents knowed that they didn't have no chance agin' me with their bare hands, because I was strong, and pretty fast."

"I seen you work a couple of times," said Buck softly. "You don't need to tell me no more about why they was afraid of you. Maybe you disremember when the five McGintys jumped us over in Five Creeks, but I ain't forgetting any too quick."

The other shrugged his shoulders, as though he deprecated such reference to his story.

"Well," said he, "what happened in Five Creeks by accident was what I was hunting dead patient for all the time when I was a kid.

"I dunno how it was, but a man cussing and swearing that he'd carve my liver out used to tickle me clean inside, and I'd ride a hundred miles to sun myself in the eyes of a gang that had swore they'd clean me up. Yes, sir, seems like it must have been another man and not Jim Conover, when I think of what I used to be and then how peaceable I am to-day."

Buck glanced up at this, blinked, and then grinned behind his hand. "Go on," said he.

"But fist fights I found out wasn't half the fun that gun fights was. It was tolerable pleasant to crack a gent across the jaw with your fist or sink your fingers into his throat like it was softsoap. But there wasn't nothing to compare with going after guns and never knowing what would happen. In a fist fight the biggest and the fastest gent was pretty sure to win if he kept his eyes open and dodged any chairs and clubs that might be coming his way. But with the guns, anything might happen.

17

"I used to practice four hours a day, part of the time, pulling a gun and turning on my heel and shooting at a mark. Or else I'd put myself in all sorts of funny positions and try myself out. I'd sit in a chair and throw a stone over my shoulder and try to jump out of that chair, lie flat on the ground, and hit the stone with a slug outn my gun before it landed on the ground."

There was a murmur of awed admiration from the little man.

"Looks like I'm trying to make myself out a famous man," said Conover. "But the facts of the matter are that the day come when I seen that I'd simply been wasting my time and worse than wasting it.

"If twenty men was talking and I came sudden into the room, they all got silent and waited for something to happen. If I passed a gent on the road, he'd gimme the right of way. If I sat down and tried to talk to somebody and pass the time of day with him, he'd freeze up like a cake of ice and lemme do all the talking. Gents that was around me used to watch every word they spoke like it might of been a slap in the face for me.

"I was so plumb mean that a couple of times when girls spoke up sassy to me, I found their men folk and took it out on 'em. The result was that every man and woman and kid around them parts was mighty careful how they handled me."

"How'd you escape being lynched?"

"Lynching me wouldn't of been so easy. Because there was my dad and all of his folks behind me, and if a finger had been laid on me, there'd of been twenty fighters come down raging out of the hills.

"That brings me bang up agin' my father. As a matter of fact, he ain't my father at all. I'm just adopted. I'm a foster child in that tribe.

"About my own father I don't remember nothing. And I disremember everything about my mother except that she was always coughing, and that her eyes was always dull and tired looking. She was traveling somewheres. She got into that part of the country and died in dad's house.

"He had three sons of his own already, but he adopted me. He said that there was always room for one cub more. The reason he took me in was because I licked one of his boys that laughed at me because I was crying over my mother. And that was how I got into his house.

"After that, he treated me the same way as he treated his own. That is, he kicked me out of the way when I was too near him and he cussed me out every time I was out of calling distance."

"What call has he got on you, then, Jim?"

"He took me in when I didn't have no ways to look for any other help, and I'd of stayed with him all this time if it hadn't been for the girl."

"Ah?" murmured Buck. "I might of knowed that there was a girl in it. What was she like?"

CHAPTER THREE

ABOUT "JACK"

"There's a time in a girl's life," said Conover, "when she strings out into mostly arms and legs and hands and feet. And that was the way with this one when I first seen her.

"That was five years ago. I guess she's growed up a lot by this time, but she was about fourteen then, and more full of angles than a snake is full of curves.

"She was as bony as an old hoss and as clumsy as a calf. Her nose was about half the size that it should have been, and there was a trail of freckles across the bridge of it. Down her back there was a pigtail of red hair, braided so hard it was like the lash of a whip.

That was the way she looked, leaving out that her eyes were big and blue and full of fire, and that her mouth and chin were made plumb careful and delicate. Can you see her, Buck?"

"Dog-gone me if she don't stand right here in front of me, I can see her that plain."

"The way I met her was in the middle of a thunderstorm. I was scooting across country hunting for cover when I seen this girl riding in front of me. There was a jag of lightning that flashed pretty close to us, and her hoss kicks up his heels and lands her out of the saddle and in the mud. I goes over and picks her up.

"Pretty soon she gets the sand wiped out of her eyes and nose and shakes the sand out of her hair like a dog.

" 'When I gets that hoss again,' says she, 'I'm going to make him wish that that lightning had hit him instead of me.'

" 'I'll bet,' says I, 'that you're plumb ferocious.'

"She frowns at me for a minute and then she gives me a grin that you could of hung your hat on.

" 'You're kind of fresh,' says she, 'but I guess you got a good heart.'

" 'What are you driving at?' says I.

" 'A kind heart,' says she, 'but simple.'

"Then I seen that she was handing me the gaff, and it warmed me up considerable, because it takes a good game one to get a tumble and come up laughing at the other man.

" 'You're a good kid,' says I, 'and you're packed right full to the ears with knowledge. But what I'd like to know is where d'you belong?'

" 'If I knew that,' says she, 'I'd start there. Do you think I'm standing here making conversation for fun? Not while this wind is blowing me to tatters.'

"I took off my slicker and offered it to her.

" 'Say,' says she, 'd'you think that I'm candy, and that I'll run and get all sticky if I'm wet?'

" 'Take this slicker,' says I, 'and stop talking about it.'

" 'What if I don't?' says she.

" 'I'll turn you over my knee and spank you,' says I.

"She looked at me for a minute so hard that I thought her eyes would snap out of her head.

" 'I presume,' says she, 'that you're joking.'

" 'That's a nice big word,' says I, 'but it don't mean no more to me than a short one. I aim to let you know that you ain't going to catch pneumonia. That ain't going to be blamed on me.'

"She keeps right on looking me over. It wasn't hard to see that she was so mad her teeth was nearly chattering. If she'd been a man she'd of blowed me higher than the sky. Dynamite was all she wanted.

" 'As a joker,' says she, 'you're a wonder. But you don't expect me to take a clown seriously. I've seen a whole circus, mister, and you're only part of one.'

"It set me back on my heels, you might say. I give her another look and begun to take her more serious. But the first thing was to make her let me put that slicker on her.

" 'Here,' says I, 'is the slicker.' And I took it off.

" 'It's interesting,' says she, 'but sort of old.'

"I caught her wrist. I didn't aim to hurt her, but in them days I didn't know my strength. She didn't say nothing, but she lost a pile of color and bit her lip.

" 'I'll put it on,' says she, as quiet as a man that knows he's beaten.

" 'Kid,' says I, while I herded that slicker around her shoulders, 'you're a game one. I'm sorry if I hurt you.'

" 'This is all in the day's work,' says she. 'But you'll be soaked to the skin in another minute.'

"The rain was sluicing down by the bucketful.

"'I got a thick skin,' says I, 'by all accounts. What's the reason you got lost?'

"'I've just come out to my uncle's ranch,' says she, 'and the lay of the land is new to me. Besides, that fool hoss had an iron jaw and went so fast I didn't see no landmarks.'"

"'What's your name?' says I.

"'The ladies call me Jacqueline,' says she, 'and the men call me Jack. The last part is Stoddard.'

"It took a good deal of the wind out of my sails, hearing that name. Old man Stoddard was the biggest rancher in them parts. Besides that, he'd always been the biggest enemy of dad and all of dad's clan.

"You see, dad and his folks had come West from the Kentucky Mountains, and they was as much of a clan in the West as they'd been in Kentucky. They had the same ways, too. They couldn't ride down to the mail boxes at the crossroads without toting along a rifle and a pair of revolvers with a knife or two stowed away convenient.

"Take 'em by and large, their idea of a quiet party consisted of a five-gallon jug of moonshine that ripped the innards out of a man. And their idea of a real good time had guns and knives in it. That was why they cottoned to me so strong. I could handle the best of 'em, and they soaked up all the credit, as they

24

called it, that come from my fights. I was their famous man, you see, and every time I raised the devil in particular, they used to sit around and tell me what a great man I was.

"I was tolerable young, and that sort of talk turns a young man's head, as you know. It made a sort of a wall that kept me from minding the opinion of all the hard-working ranchers around through the range that looked on me about like they looked on a rattle-snake.

"So when that kid told me that she belonged to the Stoddard tribe, I seen that when she knowed my name she'd be through with me. May seem strange to you, but it sure put the whip to me to think of her turning her back on me. But I decided that I'd postpone her knowing.

"'And what's your name?' says she.

"'You ain't old enough to hear such things,' says I, and with that I put her up in my saddle and started along with the hoss following me.

"'This hoss seems to like you,' says she.

"'He's a plumb simple-minded hoss,' says I, and so we go along, heading back for the Stoddard Ranch and making foolish-sounding conversation all the ways. Dog-gone me if I didn't laugh till I was weak, at the lingo that girl had. But pretty soon we come over a hill and there was the ranch house beneath us, and there I stopped.

" 'Ain't you coming in to have a cup of coffee and get your clothes dried out?' says she. 'Besides, I want my uncle to meet you. He'll be mighty grateful.'

"I had to tell her the truth then. 'If your uncle was to see me coming, d'you know what he'd do?' says I.

" 'Well?' says she.

" 'He'd call his men and tell 'em to get their guns.'

" 'Oh,' said the girl, 'if he didn't like you, he wouldn't ask for any help to meet you. The Stoddards aren't people of that sort.'

" 'You're wrong so far as I'm concerned,' says I.

" 'She started to make one of her sassy remarks, but she seen that I was serious and she got sober quick.

" 'Who are you?' says she.

"All at once it hit her. I could see the wave of understanding wash over her face and put a shadow in her eyes. She slid offn the hoss and jerked off the slicker.

" 'You're Big Jim,' says she.

" 'I am,' says I.

"She backed away from me; I could see that she half hated me and half feared me, and I knew that she'd heard all the stories about me.

The truth was bad enough, but what the Stoddards had to say made me out worse'n a man-eating tiger.

" 'I'm sorry you're in a hurry,' says I. 'But you was telling me that the Stoddards didn't have no fear.'

" 'Not of men,' says she, 'but we hate snakes.'

"And then she turned around and ran like she was being chased down the hill.

"I climbed back into the saddle and forgot all about the slicker lying there on the ground. All I could think about was the sick look in the face of that kid. It wasn't only that she was afraid of me, but something about me disgusted her.

"That was why I broke away from the gang. I left home that night without stopping to say good-by to nobody. I changed back to my own father's name of Conover, and here I am, Buck, sitting in the woods telling you about a dead part of my life. I never dreamed that I'd ever go back to it. I've never forgotten the look in Jack's face. It's kept me living pretty straight and clean for the past five years."

"The straightest in the world, Jim. But there's one thing you don't seem to dwell on none."

"What's that?"

"When you get back into them parts, what'll

27

they do to you when they find out that you can't defend yourself?"

"They'll never find it out. I can walk straight enough to keep 'em from knowing."

"They'll know when they see you eat."

"I can do that when I'm by myself."

Buck shook his head.

"If you ride home, I'm going with you. I'm going with you to take care of you."

"Partner, you ain't a gun fighter. If anything *did* start, they'd eat you up."

"I say, I'm going!"

Big Jim looked at the fire for a moment.

"If that's the way of it," he said, "I stay here."

CHAPTER FOUR

A WORTHLESS PROMISE

It was only upon this assurance that Buck fell peaceably asleep that night. With a rifle he was as good as the next man, but men could not be hunted with the cool leisure which is so necessary an adjunct of rifle shooting. Fights with men took place with the speed of thought.

The man with whom one drank one instant

might be one's opponent in a duel the next. The least chance phrase at which offense was taken, was the signal. For either to be slow, the one in giving offense and the other in taking it, was a disgrace whose stain sank deeper than any subsequent heroism could wipe out. Six-shooters were the things for such affrays, leaping out of their holsters and barking out their defiance, chopping short the sound of the last oath. And with revolvers Buck was only a very mediocre performer.

He would have accompanied Jim through any crisis, to be sure, and would have fought with all his power to avenge the fall of his companion or to prevent it. Yet he knew well enough that his special talents could not be called into play in such a game, and he was glad enough when Jim assured him that he would give up the trip to see his foster father rather than risk Buck's life.

"And after all," It's just himself, "Jim doesn't really want to go. It's just duty that's dragging him down yonder."

Upon this thought he fell asleep, and no dreams visited him during that night. When he wakened it was not from the terror of a nightmare but his eyes flashed suddenly wide, and he sat up amid his blankets. He looked across the shack to the place where Conover should be sleeping. But Conover was gone, and his very blankets had been withdrawn.

How he could have managed it without wakening so light a sleeper as Buck, the latter could not imagine. With infinite cunning and stealth it must have been done.

He leaped out and ran into the open, shouting for Conover, but the noise of the rising storm swallowed his voice. He ran back to the little meadow among the trees where the horse of Conover was kept, but the stalwart outlines of the stallion did not appear, and Buck knew that his comrade had merely given his word with the intention of breaking it; merely given his promise for the sake of lulling the suspicious anxiety of Buck, though he intended the while to leave his partner and range away for himself.

So Buck, cursing wildly, ran for his own horse, threw a saddle on him, jammed the bit of a bridle between his teeth, and rushed away through the darkness to find his lost man.

But Conover was not to be found. For one thing, Buck did not take the right direction to begin with. For another thing, he remembered after he was under way that he did not even know the location of the big man's home country.

It would be a long trail at the best, and it would be necessary to hide away the tools at the mine before he proceeded with it. He brought them out from the shaft, hid them in a deep crevice behind a stone, and next he cached away the food and started back for his journey.

He had no hesitation about leaving the mine. He would have left it as willingly with a great strike under his pick. For what he owed to Jim Conover was more than all the gold in the world could pay for.

He saddled his own horse and then ran to unpicket the burros and let them run loose to freedom, if they chose it, for it would be long before he came back to the mine. Of that he was sure.

In the telling of his tale, Conover had made only one mistake, and that was in giving the name of the girl's family. It would be for the name of Stoddard that Buck would search. But it was hard to find a single name upon three thousand miles of range, and it might be weeks before he arrived on the scene.

Long before that, Conover would have encountered his danger unaided. If Buck rode out on the trail it was not in the conviction that he could be of use, but merely in the knowledge that he must work on half blindly. He could not stand still and feel that his friend was walking calmly into danger of his life.

These were the thoughts which grew in Buck as he rode through the dark of the night forest, but he was spurring his horse in the wrong direction.

While he rode north and east to cross the range, Conover was dropping to the west down from the hills and into the plain. When the daylight found Buck still among hills to the north, it found Conover out in the heart of the desert, pushing relentlessly on through the dust.

It was a three-day ride before he came into the old country where he had spent his youth and where every hilltop had a familiar face for him. He looked upon them in this day of his return with a singular affection and some sorrow. For he felt that they would see something great in his life before long—perhaps they would witness his death.

In five years men would not have forgotten the wild deeds of his youth. The things he had done would not be forgotten, and neither would the hatred which many a score bore for him have diminished. But the fear they had felt for him in the old days would have grown small; and if they tried out his skill again, it would be the end of him at once.

There was only one thing which could help him in such an emergency. It was vain to think that his left hand had sufficient skill in it to make a quick draw and fire an accurately placed shot. He must carry this affair through with the purest bluffing.

He determined, therefore, to pass straight through the little town instead of skirting around it to get to the house of his adopted father.

However, before he passed through, he stopped his horse and transferred the holster from the left to the right side of the cartridge belt. To be sure, on the right side it was worse than useless, a mere incumbering weight, but he must keep it in this place to impose upon the eyes of the villagers.

He must try to awaken their memories and recall to them what Big Jim had been. If he could do that effectually, then he was past all danger, and they would as soon think of opposing him as of opposing an avalanche. So he cast about in his mind for a means of reintroducing himself most effectively to them.

Conover rode slowly down the street of the little town, in the meantime turning hundreds of reminiscences through his mind as he went. There was hardly a house which did not mean something to him personally. There was hardly a corner around which he had not fled from a crowd or dashed in pursuit of a single enemy. There was hardly a window from which awe-stricken eyes had not glared out at him in hatred and in fear.

He went straight to the hotel and sat down

upon the veranda, in the only vacant chair in a thick line of idlers. He was doubly right in thinking that they would not remember him. Of this entire group there was not a single familiar face.

The town had grown greatly since he was last there. His five years had changed him; and the five years had turned boys into men and put beards on smooth chins. Moreover, these were mostly cow-punchers from the neighboring ranches, and, of course, a cow-puncher population is as shifting as the sands of the desert. At least, there was not one who cast a familiar eye upon him.

But now a whisper ran up and down the line. Had some one recognized him and given out a name which, in spite of five years, must still be strong enough to raise a ghost in the mind of every man there? No, they were not glancing at him in awe, but with mischievous smiles. They expected trouble, but they expected it to come *his* way and not theirs.

Conover rubbed his chin reflectively and reached for his cigarette makings before he recalled that he must not roll a cigarette in public, for the reason that it would expose the new clumsiness in the fingers of his right hand.

A step sounded behind him, at this point,

and a hand fell upon his shoulder. He glanced up and saw that a tall young man was standing just behind his chair.

He was a magnificent fellow. He was as nobly built as Conover himself, and he was dressed like a very Beau Brummel of cowpunchers, from the shop-made boots upon his long and narrow feet to the silver-loaded band of his sombrero. A Mexican dandy would have envied him for his brilliance. He shone as though he were scattered over with bits of a mirror.

"Partner," he said calmly to Jim Conover, "I dunno that you know it, but you're sitting in my chair."

Consternation rushed across the heart of Conover. He was to be challenged this very instant before the slightest shadow of his old reputation had fallen before him. Oh, what a fool he had been to trust himself among these quarrelsome fellows. But in the meantime he must pass this test, or he was ruined indeed. He summoned all of his resolution and met the glance of the big fellow quietly enough.

"How long," said he, "have folks been reserving chairs out here on this veranda?"

"Friend," said the puncher, "I ain't interested in old customs. I like to make up my own rules. Understand?"

"That's a good custom," said Conover, "but

a gent needs a heavy life insurance to live comfortable while he tries to make his own laws."

Conover felt the start and the slight scraping of many chairs as the whole line of the idlers took note of what was passing in this dialogue. And the big man who leaned over the chair of Conover started, stared down in surprise as if he could not believe that he was challenged, and then allowed a black frown to sweep across his face.

He glanced up and down the line to make sure that all attention was centered upon him. Then he made ready to crush this insolent and overweening stranger and brush his remnants from his path.

CHAPTER FIVE

FACING A KILLER

He was in no haste, however, to execute his purpose, for Charlie Masters knew that a description of a fight is always more interesting when the action is framed with conversation, and on his powers as a conversationalist, in such a great moment, Masters prided himself. He felt that he had at his command words

36

which were whips, and when the tale of his exploits and his killings were recounted, there would be many a stirring passage at dialogue before the passages of arms.

As a matter of fact, Charlie Masters had framed his life after the pattern of certain heroes of the road of whose adventures he had read. To him it seemed that there was no nobler goal attainable by man than that of the man killer who is outlawed, and who ranges up and down the mountains preying upon the society which has cast him out simply because his prowess was unequaled.

He had not yet been cast out, but this was not because the butt of his favorite Colt was unnotched. He had killed three men with it and wounded half a dozen others more or less seriously. And all of this before his twenty-third year. But on every occasion Charlie could claim that he was simply using his best endeavor to protect himself, not deliberately attempting to do a murder.

He had often looked a jury in the face, yet the juries had been convinced by his candor and his youth, for though all actors are not necessarily rascals, all rascals are necessarily actors. He had convinced the juries, and he had escaped, and though the patience of society had been great indeed, it was now exhausted.

However, Charlie hardly cared. He would even welcome the time when it was no longer necessary to work with anything other than his guns. As he leaned above the stern face of Conover, Charlie was deciding that this must be his man.

In the first place, he would lead his stranger on into rash statements.

"Partner," said Charlie, as mildly as he could, though his voice was a more or less uncontrollable bass, "partner, you hear me asking you all polite and smooth to get up out of a chair that don't belong to you."

"Partner," responded Conover in exactly the same fashion, "if you show me a bill of sale for this here chair you're sure welcome to it."

"I was sitting in that chair," said Charlie, "which makes it mine."

"I'm sitting in it now. And I intend to stay sitting right here."

"Stranger," remarked Charlie, "I aim to let you know that you may be raising up a whole pack of trouble."

If he had not guessed it from the words and actions of Charlie, he might have known by the actions of the bystanders. For every one of the line of idlers had come out of his chair and all were assembled in a ragged group with a great gap on either side of the disputed chair so that there would be no one in direct line with flying bullets. And yet the stranger did not seem disturbed. He actually pressed on toward the danger mark.

"Young fellow," said Conover, "if you was older I'd expect you to know. But being just a kid I guess we can forgive you being fifty per cent blockhead, too. Son, you're right on the edge of the falling-off place. Get back out of my way."

After this, danger could not be increased. It was battle only that remained before them.

"Darn you," snarlingly replied Charlie, the wolf coming with a leap to the surface in him. "I'll turn you into a sieve for this, stranger. And before I do it, I want you to know the name of the gent that finished you."

"Son," said Conover, "I'll be glad to know."

"I'm Charlie Masters!"

It was a new name to Jim Conover, but he emphasized the fact that it was unknown. He rubbed his chin and seemed to study the distance with intense effort.

"Ain't ever heard that name," he declared at last. "Have you got a reputation for something, son?"

There was a faint chuckle among the bystanders. And the creaking of a rusted windmill near by seemed like a shriek of senseless laughter. Now and again, at long intervals, that wail came from the windmill irregularly.

"Stand up!" barked out Charlie. "Stand up and we'll have this out right here and now, stranger. Am I going to know the name of the gent that I finished?"

"When you get to purgatory," said Conover mildly, "ask the keeper of the gate who sent you. He'll tell you as you pass through."

It brought another chuckle from the spectators, another growl from big Charlie. Then Conover rose from his chair and confronted Masters. The hand of the latter flew to his gun, and remained there. For Conover had folded his arms as he rose, and low as Charlie Masters was, he could not take an undue advantage of the draw.

"Get your gun out," said Conover.

"Go for your own," said Masters. "I ain't no murderer."

But Conover smiled. "You fool," he said, "I'll kill you before you have the muzzle clear of the leather. But let me see you start your motion. It ain't any pleasure for me to start on an even break with a kid that ain't got a reputation. I ain't a cradle robber, no matter what else they may call me!"

It was a heavy blow to the vanity of Charlie. He blinked and winced. And his rather small, rather bright eyes glanced from side to side. After that instant of wavering he turned his

40

attention back to Conover.

"Are you going to fight, or are you going to run?" he answered sneeringly.

"Don't worry about me, son," said Conover smilingly, and all the while he was wondering how much further he could go, and how it would be possible to break the nerve of this big gun-fighter without actually drawing a weapon upon him. "Don't worry none about me. I'll do the finishing of this here argyment. It ain't the first time that I've done duty as the fool killer."

The face of Charlie Masters was blotched with two colors, just as his soul was rent with two emotions. The one color was the white of wonder and of fear. The other color was the purple red of anger. He swayed as he stood there.

"By heavens," he whispered, "get your gun out, or I'll kill you now, and be darned to you!"

There was no doubting that Masters meant business now. There might be elements of cowardice in him, as there are in almost every bully, but there was also a furious love of battle, and this was the predominant emotion now.

Conover, knowing that he was on the very brink of destruction, cast wildly about him for some means of delay and of escape. The first thought that came to him was a foolish expedient, but it must serve.

"Suppose," said he, "that we go for our guns at a signal. Now that we've agreed about everything else, and we don't want to disappoint a crowd like this that's looking for a show, suppose that we use a signal. And for a signal—say we take the next creak of that windmill?"

Masters blinked again. These delays were bringing an edge to every one of his nerves. But he dared not refuse any challenge which was delivered to him in the presence of such a group of men as watched him now. Yet, inwardly, he registered a vow that his battles hereafter would be sudden and short. One spring, and then kill or be killed. However, he must carry through with this affair.

"The first creak of the windmill, then," he agreed. "And the devil take the last man out with a gun. But—are you going to keep your arms folded?"

"Don't worry about me, Masters. You'll need any handicap I can give you!"

Once more Masters shuddered as a doubt of victory passed through his brain. But he shook his head to rouse himself. He made a movement as though to fold his arms in imitation of his enemy. But there was too much uncertainty in his brain.

Doubtless this maneuver of the stranger was a cunning trick. Besides, infinite confidence breathed out from his face and his whole manner of bearing himself. And Charlie Masters, clutching the butt of his gun, prepared for the worst. He could see, from the corner of his eye, that wonder was seizing upon the crowd, as it saw its champion grasping at every advantage and accepting the proffered handicap. But Charlie was not greatly regarding the crowd. His eyes and his thoughts were fastened upon the stranger. For it seemed as though power over life and death lay in the calm eyes of Conover. Who could guess what lay inside of them?

For to Conover there remained no hope except that he might not flinch when the revolver was drawn which was to shoot him down.

Then a new face appeared. It was old Jeff Handley, at the door of the hotel.

"It's Charlie Masters ag'in'," he called guardedly back to others inside the building. "It's Charlie Masters, and, by the eternal, it's Big Jim come back ag'in!"

The last phrase was no more than the softest of whispers, breathed forth in the deepest spirit of awe, and yet it had the effect of a knife prick at the ribs of every man near Conover. They might have grown up in ignorance of the face and the form of the famous fighter, but every one of them knew his name and his exploits. And they were frozen with excitement and dread.

"It's the end of Masters," some one murmured.

And Masters heard and agreed. His heavy jaw sagged till his mouth opened. His eyes grew suddenly dull. His shoulders stooped as though a weight had been placed upon them. And the hand which clutched the handle of the revolver shook. Plainly he was unnerved. And had that revolver of Conover's been upon his left hip, he could have drawn it with his clumsy left hand and killed his man. He knew that, and he ground his teeth with a savage regret behind that invincible smile which he was still maintaining.

Then the windmill screeched in the distance. The revolver leaped out into the hand of Masters and sparkled in the sunshine. And Conover did not stir. He was still stiffly erect. His arms were still folded. His eyes were still level. His lips were still smiling.

And it seemed as though the weight of the gun in his hand was too much for Masters. It did not speak. Instead, it seemed to unbalance him and tug him forward. He dropped heavily upon his knees. The revolver fell from his nerveless fingers.

44

"Don't shoot!" he whispered to Conover. "In the name of God, don't shoot!"

Conover stepped one pace closer. Poor Masters threw his hands before his face as though to ward off the blow, but Conover simply kicked the fallen revolver off the veranda and into the dust of the street.

"Now," he said to Masters, "get out of the town and don't forget to stay away. They know you around here now for what you are— a skunk and a coward, and if you come back here again, some kid will step up to you and wipe his boots on your face!"

And Masters, reeling to his feet, stumbled from the veranda, felt his way like a blind man around the corner of the hotel, and then broke into a staggering run which he did not cease from until he had reached his horse, saddled it, and then spurred away out of town.

No one ever heard of him again.

As a matter of fact, he changed his name, went far north, and this very day remains there as a cook in a logging camp, loved for his skill with pots and pans, but despised because God put so small a heart in so great a body.

CHAPTER SIX

THE CLAN OF MORNE

How close Big Jim himself had come to fainting no one saving himself would ever know. But the sun began a swirl of blackness before him, and his breath failed him. He had to slump back into a chair, and, whether the clumsiness of his right hand and the fact that the left did all the work was noticed or not, he had to roll a cigarette, light it in haste, and drag breaths of the nerve-restoring smoke deep into his lungs.

But his clumsiness was not noticed. There was no danger of that for the moment, at least. The crowd was walking restlessly back and forth around him. The old-timers had appeared from here, there, and everywhere, so it seemed. And they seemed almost glad to see Big Jim.

Conover knew the truth. He was like a great and famous landmark which was restored to them, and though it began a bane to them, nevertheless they were proud, in a mournful way, of the desperado who made their town famous.

"I'd ruther of seen him die with a bullet through his brain, if he had any," said old Jeff Hanley, shaking hands with the returned prodigal. "I'd ruther of seen him tore to piece by wolves than to have him finished the way he was. Dog-gone me if that wasn't the awfulest thing I ever seen in all of my days!"

"Inside of a day he'll be taking water from a Chinaman," said Hanley, and others who heard the remark agreed with it.

"You've growed old," said Hanley to Jim, trying to pump him for news. "And you must of been living in a far-off country since we last seen you down here in these parts. There ain't been a whisper of you, Jim."

"If I was to tell you what I been doing for the last five years," said Jim, truthfully enough, "you wouldn't believe a word that I tell you."

"Leastwise," said Hanley grinning, "I wouldn't call you a liar!"

Big Jim rose and laid a hand of protest on the shoulder of the hotel proprietor.

"Did you ever know me to go off hunting down an old man, Hanley?" he asked, and then strode down the veranda, conscious of his right leg, and praying that it might not drag.

His prayer was not answered. Every eye could see that there was something wrong with that right leg, but what it was no one could guess. And, besides, who could have had a brain omniscient enough to understand that there had been nothing but the power of a sham with which big Masters had just been beaten down and shamed so terribly out of his manhood.

They saw the wreck of Big Jim mount a horse and ride down the street again, and to every man in the town he was greater than ever. For in the past days, as every one knew, he had struck down fighting men with his bullets, but on this day they had seen him dispose of a warrior by the strength of his will alone. He was a mixture now of God and hero.

But Big Jim Conover, riding out of town, was still weak with the trail through which he had just passed. He had been through dangers before, but he had never before been so perilously close to infinity. At least, he had bluffed his way through the crisis, and he suspected that it would be long indeed before his prowess was actually tested in a more practical fashion, at least in that neighborhood. The tale of what he had done that day to Masters would be told and retold, and the awe of Big Jim would be restored in its pristine vigor.

So he came in sight of his adopted father's homestead. And Conover drew his horse under a tree, dismounted, and sat on a big stump to view the place where he had spent his boyhood and his youth. It seemed to have grown smaller during the past five years. And on the whole it was darker and gloomier.

It lay in a hollow, thick with trees. A creek wound obscurely to the side, and among the trees the buildings were spread. For the time and the talents of John Morne and his family had been devoted to various occupations. He had been a rancher, since coming West. He had been a hunter and trapper. He had been a miner. He had been a lumberman. And his whole clan had followed him in each of these occupations.

Indeed, so strongly felt was the leadership of John Morne that not one of his sons had broken away from the old homestead. And therefore it was that the place resembled a village more than a ranch headquarters. Scattered among the trees, were small houses, each—except for the sheds and the barns—representing a family.

He had three sons—Phil, Hector, and Bill Morne, and each of these had married and brought his family home. There was the Pattisons, too, Mat and Oliver, who had come to their uncle's headquarters to seek protection.

Their crimes were not attested by enough evidence to bring the law upon their heads, but they were well enough known to have brought them a few pounds of lead if they had ventured into the society of the range unescorted. So they came with their families to John Morne, and John took them in, knowing well that by so doing he at once alienated every man in the land against him, but nevertheless too proud to refuse help when it was asked by a blood relation.

Big Jim well remembered the night when the beating of the hoofs of horses had rattled down the valley and wakened him in his attic room. He remembered how he had pulled on his trousers and dragged down the stairs a long rifle which he could already use as well as any man. And he arrived in the front room in time to see the front door fly open and two big men dash in with mud in their beards and terror and rage in their eyes, demanding shelter from John Morne.

Before he could answer, the hoofs of other horses clattered outside, and the posse began to break in—until half a dozen leveled guns held by the inhabitants of the house warned them back again. There they stood, cramming the doorway, and told Morne that if he protected these villains his life and the lives of all who were with him would be forfeit sooner or later.

How well Jim recalled the answer of Morne: "These here men are my nephews. Blood ties

50

'em to me; it'll take death to part 'em from me. And there ain't nothing going to take 'em away except the law of the land. Where's there a sheriff in your crowd. Let him step out and ask for what his warrant names. The rest of you—scatter!"

There was no sheriff, and the rest scattered. They remained outside the house for some time, loudly discussing violent means of revenging themselves for being thus balked of their vengeance, and freely advising that the place be burned to the ground as a nest of vermin and every man in it hanged. Some wiser voice dissuaded. That was the rich rancher, Stoddard. Jim had recognized his tone and his diction.

"If you shoot down the grown men without the law on your side, spirit and letter, you'll make a scandal that'll fill the whole country. And the Morne children will grow up thinking that they've got a right to live by murder and theft.

"No, boys, we've run against a snag. The only thing we can do is to go home and wait for another time. You can trust that it will come. The day will come when the Mornes will be stamped out like vermin! All that we need is patience."

Jim had never forgotten. From that day forth, in his heart of hearts he had considered

Morne and his tribe as vermin who must one day be stamped out. Yet they still existed.

The houses were a little more dilapidated than they had been five years before. But the tribe was just as numerous. He could hear the voices of the children come up to him on the hill, like the swarming of school children in the play yard at recess. In fact, the Mornes and the Pattisons must have multiplied greatly since he had last seen them.

On what did they live? On debts, a few cattle straggling over a range of uncertain boundaries. a little hunting and trapping for skins, and on much more unsavory business which was kept from the light of day as much as possible. Yet it could not be entirely concealed, and every one knew that when long riders and hunted men of every description passed through that country they found a shelter among the clan of Morne and paid richly for it.

Every one knew, also, that gangs of raiders were many and many a time recruited from among the lean and hungry men of the hollow. Now and again the bullets of a posse brought down a Morne. But they were a race of savage fidelity to one another, and there had never been a Pattison or a Morne who would name his kin in a confession. Their pride on earth remained their pride in death.

It was of such things that Big Jim thought as he climbed again onto his horse and started down the valley. There was no doubt that the great John Morne had not yet passed away, for had he done so, there would have followed three days of unremitting wailing and weeping. The hollow would have been filled with sounds of sorrow.

He rode leisurely, therefore, down the slope and into the wood, and here, at the first turning of the path, a sharp voice challenged him.

Conover halted at once, and, turning his head, he saw to his right a mounted man, partially screened among the leaves and balancing a long rifle across the horn of the saddle. For the Mornes and the Pattisons were a rifle-loving tribe. They could wield their revolvers with enough adroitness to satisfy the most exacting, but on the whole they loved accurate rather than swift shooting, and the maxim which old John Morne had laid down long before, was that they should never shoot until they had been provoked three times, but then they should shoot to kill, and do it with a rifle.

"What's up?" asked Jim in surprise. "Might be a camp of soldiers that I'm riding toward?"

The sentinel pressed a little forward. He was revealed as a mere stripling of perhaps fifteen. But he had the big bone and the hard and sinewy muscle for which the Mornes were famous. Even now he was ready to do a man's part physically, and by the glitter in his straight-looking eyes, he was ready to do it in spirit also. He was a creature of the most finely tempered steel.

"Well, partner," said Jim, "are you here doing sentry duty?"

"You can save that funny talk," said the boy sternly. "I'm out here doing my job. If you're a friend you can start in talking friendly. If you ain't a friend it's my job to see that you get to the devil out of this here hollow, and, by the heavens, you'll see that I'll do it!"

Had it come to this, then, that the wall between the Mornes and the rest of the world was so distinctly raised that sentinels watched the lines of approach from one to the other? The Mornes were close to the end of their rope, then. A little more and there would be a flood of angry men pouring into this hollow, men in such numbers that they could afford to scorn even the terrible fighting qualities of the defenders.

"I'm mighty sorry to hear it," said Jim Conover. "I'm mighty sorry that it should have turned out this way. I see that it's the end of the gang not far away. I've come down here to see John Morne."

"What might be your business with him?"

"To find out how sick he is."

"Look here," said the boy, "I don't like what you say, and I don't like the way you got of saying it. Understand? If I was you, I'd. forget that I had any business in Morne Hollow and start traveling pretty pronto."

Big Jim smiled. "Might you be Jud Pattison?" he asked.

The other started and peered intently at Jim. But this recognition seemed to make his suspicions only the greater than they had been before. Here he heard the rush of hoofs sweeping down the hollow. At this, as though prepared to encounter even a double danger, he set his teeth till the wedges of muscle stood out at the bases of his jaw, moved his horse back a couple of paces by simply swinging his body in the saddle, and jerked up his rifle, so that it was ready for instant firing.

Now a whistle was sent forth by the approaching horseman, and at the sound of it half the alarm and apprehension in the face of the sentry disappeared. A wildly galloping rider now appeared down the trail behind Conover. Conover himself had only a glimpse of an upraised, ecstatic face of a boy no older than the sentinel who now confronted him.

As he passed, the rider shrieked forth a message which remained in the ear of Conover only as a tingling cry for an instant, and then it resolved itself into words:

"Big Jim is coming!"

It brought a whoop from the sentry that would have been worthy of a redskin indeed. Then his yell died away on his lips.

"Big Jim," he began. "Why *you're* Big Jim!"

His stern manliness deserted him. The half-frightened and wholly delighted boy tucked his rifle under one arm and extended the other hand to Jim.

"My heavens," he said, "ain't we-all mighty glad to see you, Big Jim!"

And as if to attest the truth of what he said, at that instant a wild outbreak of yelling began from the direction of the houses, and Conover knew that the tidings of his arrival had reached the whole clan of Morne.

CHAPTER SEVEN

ASSISTANCE NEEDED

He found John Morne not lying on his death bed, but sitting up beneath an apple tree in front of his house, with his hair, which he wore very long, and which was of the most shining silver, blowing about his face. And around him played the children of the clan of Morne.

There seemed to be a score of them, and they were running as fast as they could toward the chair of the patriarch, where they huddled close and looked toward the trail which wound out from the trees and into the clearing. When they saw Conover, at a signal of the raised arm of old Morne, they began a wild and silver-thin shouting of delight and rushed across the open space toward the rider. The great horse picked his way carefully among them, shaking his head at their noisy choruses, and putting down each foot with the care of a great cat walking over damp ground. So they came to Morne, and Conover dismounted and found himself instantly up to the waist among dancing children with their jubilant hands waving in his face.

Jim Conover scooped up two in either arm and lifted them high.

"What the devil is all this noise about?" He asked them.

"You've come to save us. You've come to keep us safe!" they shrilled at him in response.

He put them back among their fellows, carefully, and then he stood over Morne. "Send them away!" he commanded.

The answer of Morne was a single outward

sweep of his hand, and the children obediently scattered away to the edge of the clearing. He raised his hand, and all their voices were hushed.

But the children were not alone. Others were coming among the trees. Conover saw men and women running, and then pausing among the trunks and waiting until the conference of Jim and the old chief should be terminated before they swarmed out. They were tremendously excited. That could be told by their hasty and irregular gestures and the hum of their murmurs.

Conover was astonished. In the old days, he remembered, the authority of John Morne had been absolute enough, but there had never been a time when a word and gesture had such strength to control all his clan.

There could only be one suitable explanation, which was that the pressure of extreme and intimate danger had forced them into a state of war when the word of the commander was most absolute. Now they hung back waiting until they were bidden to advance.

"So it was all a sham," said Conover, by way of greeting to John Morne. "That letter about the deathbed was all a fake to get me down here into the trap with the rest of you, John Morne?"

The white and bushy eyebrows of the old

man lifted. "There was a time when you called me father, or dad, Jim. You've put them names behind you, eh?"

"I've put them names behind me," said Conover sternly.

"I ain't asking you why, Jim."

"No, you can guess fast enough."

"But some folks would say that I had a right to be grieved, Jim."

"Some folks would, but you got more sense than that."

"What of all the years that I kept care of you, Jim, when you was a helpless kid?"

"What of the money that I made and turned in to you, Morne?"

The old man shrugged. "Are you keepin' account of that agin' me?"

"Not if you'd taught me to make that money fair and square by honest work, Morne. But you made a man killer and a thief out of me. You took me in, but you took me in just to make a crook out of me."

Morne stirred a little uneasily in his chair. "I treated you no worse than I treated my own kin, Jim. When everybody's hand was agin' me, how could I teach my boys to make a living fair and square by honest work?"

Conover bit his lip and then repressed the words which had tumbled up against his teeth.

"Let that go," he said. "Why did you send for me?"

"Because I needed you most terrible and most quick, Jim!"

"And why?"

"The jig was almost up with us. They're closing in fast, Jim. About a year back this here thing happened."

He was wrapped in a long slicker which he now brushed to one side and exposed his legs. His right leg was missing from the knee down."

"After that happened," said John Morne, "it ain't been so easy for me to get about and look to the affairs of the family."

"How did it happen?"

"There was a little trip over to the town of Two Falls, and when we was coming back a spent bullet hit me here in the calf of the leg. I didn't think nothing much of it; just tied it up. But it got infected and swelled up. When we got to a doctor, he had to slice it off at the knee, and I ain't sat a hoss ever since."

"You'd been making a raid," said Conover.

The old man nodded. "We got to live," he said. "I been looking around for a leader to take my place, and there ain't anybody but you, Jim. That's why I sent for you!"

"Where's Phil? Ain't Phil able to lead?"

"Phil's where we all got to go."

"He's dead?"

"Phil is dead. God have mercy on his soul, poor Phil is dead."

"There's Hector and Bill. Why not one of them?"

"Hector is with Phil, and Bill is serving time. He got a ten-year sentence, and there's still seven year to run on that term."

Conover drew a great breath. It was exactly as he could have suspected, but it shocked him to the heart to hear these things. No matter what he felt about the worth of these men, he had grown up with them, he had tumbled and fought and played with them.

"And there's nobody else?"

"Nobody that the boys will follow. And there ain't much left except kids, Jim. You must of been stopped coming down the trail by one that's as old and as good in a pinch as any of the rest of 'em."

"Young Pattison?"

"Yep."

"You mean to say that the folks around here would make a fight agin' kids like him?"

"They would. They hate us, Jim. They've always hated us. And sometimes I think that if they got a chance at us, they'd murder the women and the children along with the rest. Me they'd burn alive, and the rest of 'em they'd shoot. That's the way they feel about us. Like we was wolves!"

"And what are you?" asked Jim bitterly.

"What chance have I had?" asked Morne. "What chance did they give me? By my rights I'd ought to of had all of the range where Stoddard now runs his cows. I'd ought of had that, but he beat me out of it, him and his crooked lawyers."

He spoke with a savage bitterness, referring to a shadowy claim which he had once put forward to an immense tract of land, basing his claim upon the misty authority of an old Spanish land grant. Conover remembered it well. All the body of the law as well as common sense was on the side of Stoddard, but Morne had thought upon the case for so long that he had become convinced that justice had been turned against him.

"It's easy enough to keep the law," said Morne, "until the law is used for a club to beat you down. Then you got to make laws of your own. That's what I done. And that's why every man's hand has been turned agin' me. And when I raised you up, I raised you the best that I could, thinking of all them things, Jim. I raised you the best, and I loved you, Jim, like you was one of my own blood."

He sighed as he spoke, and the heart of Conover began to melt. It was doubtless nine tenths a lie, but the lies of old Morne were ever as convincing as the truth on the lips of another man.

"So I'm to be the commander—under you, Morne?"

"That's it, Jim. Without you, they'll wipe us out. They'll butcher the poor boys. But with you, there ain't going to be no bloodshed. They'll be afraid to lay a hand on any of us."

Conover smiled grimly. "It's no good," he said. "It simply won't work, and even if I was willing to do the work, I ain't able to."

"You not able to? Just after cleaning up Masters without even the use of a gun?"

"If I'd had to use more'n that bluff I couldn't of done it. You got half a leg gone, but I'm worse than you."

And so, briefly, he told how the explosion in the mine had crippled him with a partial paralysis. Morne listened with a face which turned purple with anger and impatience. There was no sympathy for the blow which had crushed Conover. There seemed, indeed, to be little more than fury because he had humiliated himself in vain before Conover.

But before the story was over he was frowning again over a new plan.

"Jim," he said, "if you bluffed 'em out once, could you bluff 'em out ag'in?"

"The next time they'd see through me."

"You're wrong. They'll never test you."

"Do you think that? Suppose that I go to the sheriff and make a proposition for him to make for us to the big ranchers. If they'll find work for our men—honest jobs—I'll answer that they'll keep the law. If they won't give our men an opening, then I stay here to lead 'em."

"That," said Morne sadly, "is half a surrender, but the time has come when we can't hold out much longer."

CHAPTER EIGHT

DOCTOR AYLARD ARRIVES

Perhaps it was that the nerves of the town had been too badly shattered by the exploit of Big Jim the day before, and by the knowledge that he was now back among his kin and that all the clan of Morne and Pattison had gathered around him, rejoicing as around a savior.

But certainly when Doctor Clinton Aylard arrived, the eyes which were cast upon him were anything but favorable. They gazed upon him as wolves might gaze upon a sheep, not too strongly fenced away from their teeth. It was not a question of whether or not they should fall upon him, but rather of who should have the privilege.

And it must be admitted that the doctor's manner was irritating. He wore no monocle, and yet he had a sort of eyeglassed air of superiority. Even his few intimates in the East found that manner unpleasant; to a Westerner it was simply maddening.

But under the social veneer he was a magnificent specimen. He was as tall as Jim Conover, and as heavily built. Moreover, his clothes were padded out with muscle, not with mere flabby flesh.

He had in his arms the strength and the science to stroke a triumphant eight and to win fame for himself as an amateur boxer. He had in his legs the power to drive himself down a football field, throwing one half of the bleachers into rapture and the other half into despair.

He had done all of these things, and more. He was an excellent swimmer, a skater, huntsman, mountain climber, and, as he himself would have put it, he was a bit of an aëronaut also. For a time, such exploits had been sufficient to satisfy him, until, one day, he graduated from his medical school and took a trip to England.

There, in the old village of Great Tokebun,

he came upon his own past. He found an old church with a smoldered Norman tower at one end and a crumbling vestry at the other, and sunk in the pavement of the church, he found a brass along whose edge ran the obscured and time-worn legend which told the world that an Aylard lay buried there.

The head of Doctor Clinton Aylard swam. He rushed back to London, quite forgetful of the green hills of England and the purple ones of Scotland, and all the fun which awaited him among them with gun or rod in hand. In London he shot cablegrams across the Atlantic to an old aunt who knew the family history. Where her knowledge failed he picked up the dim trail in libraries here and there, and at length he had unraveled, or felt that he had unraveled, the whole mystery.

He traced his family history back to the year 1625, when a certain youngest son bearing the name of Aylard had sailed abroad, and, after sundry adventures in the West Indies, had landed in Virginia. And if this were really the root of the American family, then he, Clinton Aylard, was really a descendant of an English earl.

For three months he read the history of the Aylards with the most frantic zeal. And when he perused accounts of how an Aylard had landed at Pevensey in the train of the conqueror, he grew sick with joy. And when he learned how that wise king, the first Henry, had made an Aylard a viscount, it filled Doctor Clinton with such a respect for and gratitude to royalty that when the king's automobile passed him in the street the next day he dragged off his hat to it, and the tears ran into his eyes.

But in the midst of these discoveries and this joy, he found that his money supply was shrinking to the vanishing point. He sold some of the clothes for which he had paid a small fortune, and boarded a steamer back for the States. In New York he found a letter from Aunt Mary Stoddard, inviting him to go West.

She was not really his aunt. Her connection with him was almost strange and romantic enough to be included in the Aylard family history. His father, Joseph Aylard, had once loved and been loved by Mary. But they had a lovers' quarrel which developed into such a breach that eventually she married, out of pique rather than affection, John Stoddard. Aylard married another woman.

Perhaps they grew to love their families well enough, but something remained untouched in them that had been touched before. When Joseph Aylard died, Mrs. Stoddard came and wept frankly over his grave and over the shoulder of his big son. She mothered him as well as she could while he was two thousand miles away, and now, in her letter, she opened her heart to him.

She was dying with heart trouble. The very hour of her death could almost be foretold, and it left barely time for Aylard to come to her while life was still in her body.

There was one great purpose which she wished to accomplish before she died, and that was a sort of secondhand substitute for her uncomplete love affair with Joseph Aylard. In a word, she wished to see her daughter, Jacqueline, betrothed to Joseph's son before she closed her eyes for the last time.

"Jacqueline," she wrote, "is a strong-headed child, but she will not resist my wish when I am on my deathbed. And you, Clinton, will find it easy to love her, for every one does.

"It will be a happy day for my husband, too. The ranch cannot be handled by a woman, of course, and he wishes to see Jacqueline married to the man who is to own the ranch as soon as possible. It is quite a great property, as you know, particularly since the oil was found; and John is eager to see it in the right hands. No hands can be better than yours, my dear, so come at once and see Jacqueline and to see me unless your heart is already entangled in another affair."

There was much more in the letter, but this was the gist of it. And Clinton Aylard studied over it for a long time. All the call of instinct, as he told himself, was to marry some English girl with a past which stretched back in an unbroken line to the days of the Conquest.

Yet there were many difficulties. To rebuild the old Aylard estate was one of the first and greatest ambitions of the new life which had opened before him. And to do this he needed money. He needed money also to lead the life of a gentleman. The great blot upon his character, he felt, was that title of doctor for which he had labored so many foolish years. But he would erase that title as soon as possible. In the meantime, here was a considerable fortune waiting for his taking.

As for Jacqueline Stoddard, she could not be the daughter of her mother without possessing a certain share of her good looks. Looks, of course, were a minor consideration. Blood was the only thing which really mattered. But in this degenerate age money was certainly a great convenience, to say the least, and Aylard felt, in conclusion, that the sacrifice must be made.

After all, it had been done before. It was not the first time that a title had been sold for

American millions. And if he had not a title, he had something just as good. He had the right to one.

So he bought a little automatic to meet conditions in the West as he might find them, dropped it into his hip pocket, and boarded a train, preceded by a telegram which announced his coming.

Aylard should have been met punctually at the train, but John Stoddard was late for it, and it was in the interim that the town looked the doctor over and decided that he would not do.

Then Stoddard came in a cloud of dust, literally. Out of the dust flashed two bays, shining and blackened with sweat. Behind them a narrow-bodied carriage danced over the bumps. In the seat of the rig sat a man well advanced through middle age, with long, iron-gray mustache drooping past his mouth, a wide-brimmed hat perched upon his head, and one closely booted leg hanging over the edge of the buggy. This was John Stoddard.

He greeted Aylard by spitting in the dust, and extending a work-hardened hand.

"Hop in, son," he said. "Sorry I'm late, but that darned off mare—hey, you, Susie, you darned little fool, you! That Susie, she ain't got a bit of sense. Seen an old whited stump a ways back up the road and dog-gone me if she didn't think it was a knot of rattlesnakes, or something like that; and by the time I got the pair of 'em stopped running, they'd drug me clean out of the way for the station."

Doctor Aylard murmured that the delay made no difference, and then got carefully into the seat beside the old rancher. But care was useless, for there was dust everywhere. It silted down his neck and up his sleeves. It whirled above his head and began to settle in a gray coat over his face. He felt that more than half of his dignity was impaired at once.

But the dust was the smallest of his concerns. The picture that had rushed upon his brain was of a mansion in England to which he had brought his American wife, and of a visit paid to them by this tobacco-chewing, wrinkle-necked ruffian, who was to be his father-in-law. Beads of cold terror joined the perspiration on his brow. He drew a great breath and choked himself with dust.

They drove to the hotel and general merchandise store, for Stoddard announced that he had to buy some collars for work horses. To Aylard it was indescribably degrading that the father of his wife to be should be interested in work of any kind, even horses. But his future father-in-law was never to dismount from the buggy to make that purchase. For as they sat in the rig just at the hitching rack, they saw a big man dismount from a magnificent horse in front of the hotel and walk across the veranda.

Stoddard touched the arm of Aylard and whispered, and Aylard listened in wonder and awe. For it was not in the books that such a man as Stoddard should whisper, even in a church.

"By the Eternal," he murmured, "that's Big Jim!"

Aylard looked again at the tall man, the wide, athletic shoulders such as he would have feared on a football field, and the seamed face which told of a life lived fast and furiously.

"Who's Big Jim?" he asked of the other, as he stared at Conover.

"It's Jim Morne," said Stoddard. "And of all them that have hit the high spots around these parts, there's no one to compare with Big Jim. He's one of them kind that can't miss a shot. He's one of them kind that don't have to shoot to kill, because they can shoot to drop. That's the way with Big Jim."

"A gun fighter such as the books tell about?"

"No book could tell about a gent like him. You got to see him in action before you understand. I've seen him work."

He said it with a sort of awe which made the doctor smile in spite of himself.

"You mean," said Aylard, "that his work

72

with a gun is very fast?"

"Lightning," said the rancher reverently. "Plumb chain lightning, when he makes a move for a gat, and straight as though he was shooting at a target."

"And yet," said the doctor, "he seems a little crippled on the right side."

For he had noted the trailing right foot as the other walked.

"Sure. Maybe he hurt that leg riding lately."

The doctor looked again. That limp had nothing to do with bumps and bruises, so far as he could make out. It was a strange thing to watch, as though all of the nerves in the limb were partly asleep.

"Look hard and fast," said the rancher. "For in my eyes there's the greatest man with a gun that ever stepped, bar none."

And he added with a sigh: "And him that downs Big Jim is sure going to be a famous man."

The doctor said nothing. But he thrust out his jaw and said to himself that if fame were to be gained by the conquest of Big Jim Morne, he, Clinton Aylard, would be the heir to that reputation.

CHAPTER NINE

UNDYING FAME

For what the rest of the town had seen and not known the meaning of, he as a physician had well understood. For there was no lameness which could account for that singular dragging and fumbling step. There was no accident which could explain the uncertain movements of the right arm and hand.

There *was* an explanation, and what it was he knew very well. It was a partial paralysis or its equivalent. The nerves on all the right side of the body were indeed partially asleep. And of that partial sleep he meant to take advantage.

Now that hunger for notoriety which had dogged him in college recurred. The old passion to bring himself into the public eye began to burn, and he told himself that there was one ready way in which he could establish himself at once.

If there were the affection of a lady to be won, in what readier manner could it be done?

"What has he done lately?" he asked.

"Lately?" said the rancher.

"Inside the past year?" asked Aylard.

"He hasn't lived near here," said the rancher. "But only yesterday morning he did the coolest thing that we've ever seen, any of us."

The hopes of Aylard diminished, but the rancher immediately went on to explain what the deed had been. It was all pure bluff, so it seemed, and as a result of that bluff a young fellow of sorts had been crushed completely.

The doctor could understand. How well he understood he dared not tell his companion. But he knew what force of courage it had required for a man who was without the full command of nerve and muscle to face an antagonist of the quality of Masters.

He asked for further particulars, and by the time they had been given, he knew why Big Jim had stayed to face out the trial. It was the last effort of an old warrior to hold his face against odds. At the moment, as Aylard could tell by the words and the manner of the rancher, Big Jim had regained his full ascendancy as strongly as it had ever existed.

The town and all of the community was under his thumb, and not a man, even of the bravest, would dare to raise his voice against the old hero.

But he would show them! He laughed when he thought what an easy task it would be.

That gun, worn upon the right hip, made him absolutely safe. A weapon worn upon the left side might have had some meaning, but he knew well enough that a gun upon the right hip was as worthless as though it had been made of wood. All that it could have been used for was as show alone. It was a part of that magnificent sham with which the old gun fighter had forced himself back upon the village. And how much it meant to Big Jim he well knew.

A man with wooden guns, so to speak, had dared to face a hundred enmities, and so far he had conquered. In a way, it took the breath of Aylard. It made him almost ashamed.

He had shown courage enough a hundred times, from the football field to the hunter's saddle, but he could hardly imagine such an exhibition of cold nerve. It was a pity to draw the mask from the face of such a magnificent rascal. But there was fame waiting for the doctor. And he intended to take advantage of the opportunity. He recalled once, when he was playing opposite a famous guard, picking out a weakened knee and falling across it until the poor devil had crumpled under the attack.

That famous day had first established the name of Aylard as a football player of the first class. Every metropolitan daily had hailed him as the hero who had crushed the famous

Thomas, and though Thomas never again appeared on the field that season, his last, it was not believed that bad condition had anything to do with his failure. It was believed that the beating he had taken at the hand of Aylard had finished him once and for all.

Aylard saw, in the weakness of Big Jim Morne, another such opportunity, and he was hungry to take advantage of it. He had gone through the rest of his college days as a football player on the strength of that one day's play against Thomas. No opposing quarter back dared to send plays through his position. He had escaped almost scot free through the thick of it.

Now he felt that if he could down Big Jim Morne in the day of that hero's weakness, he would be established once and for all as a warrior par excellence, and no lesser men would dare to challenge him.

"It seems to me," he said to the rancher, "that it's a shame a fellow like that can bully the whole town. I should think that one man would be strong enough to stand up to him and to hold him off, just for the sake of the sport of the thing!"

There was the faintest of sneers upon the lips of the rancher. He answered coldly: "I've heard gents talk up just the way that you're doing. But when it come to a pinch they lost their nerve, and they understood darn well why it was that Big Jim didn't have much trouble running the town. I ain't a coward myself, but I'd as soon face a machine gun as to face Big Jim in a fight. It wouldn't be a fight, it would be suicide."

The whole speech could not have been better designed to please the doctor. He swallowed his smile.

"I've half a mind," he said, apparently half to himself, "to get out and take a hand with this fellow."

"I ain't holding you," said the rancher. "I believe in every gent making his own way in this old world of ours."

The doctor sprang out of the buggy.

"Wait a minute," said the rancher. "Don't be a darned fool. See that gent he's talking to now?"

"Well?" asked the doctor.

"That's the sheriff."

"What about him?"

"There ain't a harder fighting man in the West than our sheriff. And there ain't a gent that'll take less offn a gun fighter. But you see him grinning and nodding with Big Jim Morne?

"It comes out of two things. The first thing is that Jim is sure death in a fight, and there ain't no mistake about that. The second thing is that in spite of him being a Morne there's something about him that's got to be respected. Sometimes it don't seem like *he could* be one of that bad blood. Well, old son, if the sheriff can afford to speak white to him, the rest of us don't need no excuse for speaking darn small around Big Jim."

"Thank you," said the doctor. "I understand what you mean perfectly. But, in my boyhood, I was taught never to buckle under to another fellow until he'd proved that he was the better man."

This would have rested well enough, but he chose to add: "And I've never yet met the better man, Mr. Stoddard."

The comparison which was beginning to blossom in the face of Stoddard disappeared under a cloud instantly, and he scowled upon his companion.

"As I said before," he announced, "there ain't anybody that can take his schooling from another man. Besides, Jim wouldn't aim to hurt a greenhorn."

He spoke the last more or less to himself. But the doctor, in the meantime, had turned away from the buggy and was sauntering toward the sheriff, and the sheriff's companion.

"I beg your pardon," he said as he came up to the pair, "but haven't I heard something about a man named Big Jim Morne who lives in this neighborhood?"

The sheriff and Big Jim turned upon him.

"Maybe you have," said the sheriff.

"I've heard that he's an unmitigated rascal and murderer," said the doctor, "and I've become curious to meet the fellow face to face. I wonder if you can tell me where he's to be found, sheriff?"

Two curious things happened at that instant. The first was that the sheriff, a man without fear, turned pale. The second was that Big Jim Morne turned his back upon the man who had just insulted him to his face and walked away.

Yet, in the next instant, the meaning of this maneuver was understood. He had turned his back so that he might swallow his wrath. He had no will to turn his gun loose upon a tenderfoot who might be forgiven on account of the fullness of his ignorance.

"Son," said the sheriff, "you've just dodged dying by a fraction of an inch. Go home and say your prayers."

"What d'you mean?" asked the doctor gravely.

"I mean," said the sheriff, pointing after Conover, "that there goes the gent that you just named."

It was very spectacular. No one who saw it

could deny that, and many saw it. The doctor walked directly after Big Jim Morne and clapped a hand upon his shoulder. Big Jim whirled upon him, but still he refrained from drawing a gun.

"Well?" asked Big Jim.

"Did you hear me say your name?" asked the doctor gravely.

"I heard it," said Big Jim.

"Then," said the doctor, "what I want to know is: Are you a cowardly dog?"

"You fool," said Big Jim, "are you hunting for a short way of dying?"

"Bah!" sneered the doctor. "I've heard a great deal about you and your ways. But I'd like to see a man killer in action. Now is your time to start, Morne."

And with that he swung his hand from the hip and cuffed Big Jim heavily across the face. So strong was the blow that Big Jim reeled back with an oath. And then, of course, the tragedy happened.

No one could understand afterward exactly what happened. All agreed that the gun of Big Jim must have stuck a little in the holster, and the draw of the doctor was a magnificent thing to see.

He stepped back, laughing. With a gesture of the utmost indifference he whipped out an automatic pistol, and still laughing, he fired before Big Jim could get his gun clear of the leather. The great gun fighter went down for the first time in his life.

The doctor kicked the gun from the hand of the fallen warrior.

"Here you are, sheriff," he said. "I think that you've been wanting this murderer even more than I have."

And he turned to face the staring eyes and the gaping mouth of John Stoddard in the buggy. He knew, by that look, that his fame was made, and would never die.

CHAPTER TEN

PLEASANT SURPRISES

If the heavens had opened above the town and an angel had appeared in a bright cloud of fire or rolling smoke, it would not have been more astounding to the townsfolk, to the rancher, Stoddard, or to the grave sheriff.

It was not only wonderful. It was horrible also, after a fashion. Just as it is horrible to see a lion bearded by a dog and backed into a corner.

That Big Jim should actually have gone down in fair fight with another man was not altogether undesirable. It would be a death blow to the ruffian Mornes. But that he should have been beaten by a stranger, a tenderfoot, and beaten with a careless and contemptuous ease was a thing that made the blood of good Westerners boil.

Big Jim was not killed. But he was stunned so completely that he did not recover from the blow for hours. When he opened his eyes and looked up from beneath the bandage which was tied around his head, the first thing that was asked was what had happened, and if his revolver had stuck in the holster. But to the queries he returned no answer, and silence could only be interpreted as a confession of a fair defeat.

But in the meantime, the doctor had become a famous man. As he climbed into the buggy to sit at the side of the rancher, it was noted by the gaping bystanders that his color had not altered, that his eye was calm, and that the smile upon his lips was not forced. These were things to tell one's children and one's grandchildren. They were unbelievable. History had indeed been made that day.

As for John Stoddard, he was crushed. He had already made up his mind about the newcomer. He had decided that even if it were to make the last moments of his wife miserable, he would not see his daughter pledged to marry this outlander, this "dude," this fine-speaking, soft-handed fellow of leisure. No matter that he was big and well made.

Quality and not quantity was what Stoddard demanded in a man, and he would rather have died than see his ranch descend into the possession of such a man as this.

And, having made up his mind, what he hated most in the world was to have to change it again. It was far easier for him to give the teeth out of his head than to surrender his opinions. Yet, within three minutes, he found that the ground of his judgment had been shattered beneath his feet.

He had to struggle hastily to readjust his thoughts, and that was what reduced him to silence. He could only give the bays their heads for an instant and let them dash down the street of the village and into the open country beyond. Once there, with the alkali dust stinging his nostrils, and the brown hills rolling away to the horizon mists, he could breathe and think again.

What he said first was: "Aylard, where in the name of the devil did you learn to handle a gun like chain lightning?"

"I've rather gone in for shooting, you know," said Aylard, and seemed to take no further interest in the conversation.

Again the rancher was dumfounded. That a

tenderfoot should have done such a deed was marvelous enough. But that he should not start talking about it at once and never stop was prodigiously strange. The doors of Stoddard's mind were wrenched ajar, and the new conception entered.

Aylard, whatever else he might be, was a man, and a man of parts. The thing he had done was of Homeric proportions. But the manner of the doing was even greater and finer. If he had rather seen his daughter dead than married to such a man the moment before, he now declared to himself that Aylard was the man of all men that he wished to become her husband.

For Stoddard worshiped physical force. He had come West when life was a fierce battle, and when only strong men could succeed, and Stoddard made himself small and humble in the seat beside his new companion.

When they reached the borders of his great ranch, he addressed Aylard with remarks about the cattle they passed and the qualities of the soil and the tales which had grown up around each section, and his manner was rather that of one partner to another than of a host to a guest.

Already he saw Aylard installed as the prospective heir to the property. But still the manner of Aylard was, in the opinion of the rancher, perfect. For he listened attentively, spoke an intelligent word now and again, and then was silent; certainly there was no gloating in his eye or his voice.

As a matter of fact, Aylard was at first amazed and disgusted. It was his first visit to a big ranch, and he was astonished to see that what he understood to be a great and flourishing property exposed to the eye only a long succession of sunburned hills sparsely covered with withered grass.

Here and there lean-ribbed cattle moved, slowly, working industriously at the dead grass, with dust in the hollows of their shoulders and along their backs—cattle which seemed on the verge of sinking down on their thin legs and resigning the battle for existence.

The white heat of the sun flashed back from the road and curled in under the brim of his hat. He could feel the lower lids of his eyes scorching. His throat closed with thirst, and the cool vision of English hills rolled back upon his memory to make him curse the great West and all that was in it.

But by degrees his mind changed. If the land did not seem rich, yet there appeared to be no limit to it. Sometimes, as far as his eye could reach, there was not a fence. And all that he saw belonged to the grim-faced man who sat beside him. And ever there was this sparse dotting of cows. Yes, there was wealth here, he began to comprehend. Besides all that he saw, there was oil, and oil meant millions, now and then. Perhaps it meant this now.

After all, he did not intend to live in the country even if he married the girl and succeeded to the estate. Once he had her in his pocket as a pledge that the ranch was to be his, he would be off to England with her to teach her to become a lady after his own conceptions.

When the father died and the estate was his, he could sell the place and live on the interest of a well-invested capital. Then for England always, England and nothing more. He would found there a great family.

Aylard House should rise from its ruins, more beautiful and more spacious than ever. The stables should open their arms to receive thoroughbred men. The bright dream raised a singing spirit to his lips, and if he listened in quiet patience to the droning and nasal monotone of Stoddard, it was because he heard the rancher with only one small corner of his mind.

They topped a hill and dipped into a hollow. There was the ranch house, and it was a pleasant surprise to Aylard.

"What the devil!" burst from his lips before he could control them.

Stoddard chuckled. "Ain't what you expected, eh?" he said. "That's Mary's doings. Dog-gone me if she ain't a surprising woman, too."

For his wife, good lady, had made a little paradise there in the hollow. An immense artesian well, bored among the hills, gave her the needed water. And with water the desert sand gave forth trees and flowers and lawns in profusion.

The hollow was rimmed about with a hedge. Behind the hedge were the lawns, with flower gardens here and there. There were trees, also, most of them transplanted so that they looked as if they had stood for two generations, and they gave an air of mellowed age to the whole scene.

In the heart of the green lawns, set about with cottonwood trees, was the house itself—not a sunwracked and unpainted frame shack staggering from the winds of the last winter, but a solid structure of concrete and dobe. Climbing vines twisted around the wide and deep casements, made patterning of green against the white walls, and climbed onto the red tiled roof. The whole house, indeed, was drenched in greenery. The very sight of it was like water in the throat of the doctor, and he decided that existence was once more a possibility even in the middle of the desert.

They passed the hedge, and they wound down a road past lawns from which cool, moist odors of grass and ground blew to them. They came nearer to the house. It was far taller and longer than it had seemed from the distance when the great trees had dwarfed its roof line. It was of one story only, and that one story was so lofty that visions of long and high-ceilinged rooms sprang into the brain of Aylard. And those thick walls would sure keep out the heat of the summer, the cold of the winter. The blue shutters were symbols of the peace which must reign within.

They whisked through a wide gate and into a spacious patio, with the road circling in and out around a central fountain and a little water garden in the midst of the place, while beyond it was the cool shadow of an arcade, thick and yet not ungraceful pillars of dobe holding up the roof.

The doctor alighted nimbly. If cruel circumstance forced him to reside for some time in this deserted land, at least he would not be without some comforts of civilization.

A negro took the horses and led them away. They passed into the house, and, the instant they were within the shadow, enchantment fell upon the mind of the doctor. He was never to see that interior exactly as it was, but all in a rosy light of make-believe. For as they passed through the first door a thrilling soprano voice ran upon his ear in the dimmer distance, singing a tune from the Beggar's Opera:

"Every night we'll kiss and stray—
Over the hills and far away!"

The music stepped suddenly closer with the middle of that line, as though a door had opened and brought the singer nearer. Footfalls scurried; a lumbering Newfoundland puppy turned the corner of the room at full speed, and just behind it raced the girl who was to be the lady of the doctor's heart.

He knew it the instant he saw her. The sweetness of her singing was still like a smile on her lips. But of the rest of her features he saw nothing, knew nothing.

It was not until later that he was to remember that her weather-brown face was framed with glorious, copper-red hair that had life of its own even through the shadows. Whether her eyes were gray or blue he could not tell. For the first time in his life he was not aware how a woman he met was dressed.

As a matter of fact, she was in a khaki riding skirt with a sombrero pushed well back on her head. But the one thing that the doctor knew was that she was beautiful, that she was wonderful, that God had made her for him.

He was not a particularly good man, this Doctor Aylard. Perhaps to few are given such cool dissimulation, such entire selfishness, an egoism so immense that it makes the individual greater than the world he lives in. But even a bad man may love with a strong-hearted fervor. And so it was that he loved Jacqueline with his first glance of her and continued to love her more than his life until he lost it.

And when she stopped short at the sight of them and he was presented, he was able to speak to her the only honest words he had spoken in many and many a day to any human being.

He took one of her slender brown hands in both of his own.

"I am a very happy man," said Aylard.

And there was so much in his voice that the girl blushed, and the rancher blushed also. It filled the cup of his happiness. For he knew that if Aylard married his daughter it would not be on account of her money.

CHAPTER ELEVEN

A BULLET THAT KILLED

They went at once into the sick chamber with the girl. There the doctor saw at a glance that Mrs. Stoddard was indeed, as she had told him in that letter, little better than a dead woman. The fallen lines of her throat, the sunken eyes, the transparent light on the forehead, and the unfleshed hands which lay upon the sheet at her breast were all the signs which tell that the spirit has already passed into the strange horizon between life and death.

Yet there was still a rare life and charm in her. Even now it seemed odd that she should have mated with such a plain and matter-of-fact fellow as the rancher.

She gave her hand to Aylard. The movement was slow, the hand itself was chill, and the touch sent a mortal coldness into his blood, yet she answered his clasp with a firm pressure. Her eyes kindled. The smile brought back a sunlight beauty to her face. It was like a fragrance of long-dead roses from an opened drawer, a thing delicately sad and lovely.

The doctor took home to his heart this pleasing sensation of melancholy, for he was an exquisite connoisseur of all emotions; he tasted of every one, but overindulged in none. To him this was no more than a well-set stage, a correctly interpreted part; and that he was admitted behind the footlights as one of the leading actors was not the least satisfying thought.

If there were a predominant idea in his mind at that instant, it was a gratitude to Mrs. Stoddard for the good taste she was showing in her death. For having prepared himself against tears, groanings, sentimental speeches, he was immensely relieved to find that these agonies were to be spared him.

When she spoke, after a little interval in which she had considered him gravely and tenderly, her voice was weak, to be sure, but quite steady.

"You are not like Joseph," she told him. "You haven't his brow or his eyes. But you have his shoulders, Clinton."

She closed her eyes; Aylard was correctly silent.

"Are you feelin' strong, mother?" asked the rancher, coming closer.

The doctor flashed a warning glance at Stoddard, but could not catch the other's eye.

"Very strong, dear," she told her husband, "and very happy. Come close to me."

He stood beside her and held her hand.

"And you?" she asked him.

That quiet voice masked a deep anxiety which drained the color from her cheeks. The doctor watched it curiously. It was like the falling of a flame in the throat of a lamp. In another instant there might be darkness. He was too impersonally interested in the scene to warn Stoddard in frank words that his wife was on the very verge of death.

"I'm happy, too," said Stoddard. "Mighty happy. And it looks to me like what you want is going to be the best all around."

The color poured into the wan cheeks of the sick woman again.

"I want to tell you about him," began Stoddard.

"Hush," she murmured.

Then she opened her eyes and looked straight at the ceiling.

"While I am still among you," she said in a louder voice, "I wish to see one great thing done for me. There has hardly been time for them to see one another. But young people do not need a great deal of time. The first glance is usually enough. For your part, Clinton, I know that you would not have come these many miles to see me if you had not decided to do what I have asked you. Am I right?"

He turned to the girl. Her smile was gone.

Something told him that the hand which was on the farther side of her, concealed from him, was clenched tightly. But she stared fixedly upon the face of her mother, and Aylard knew two things suddenly, completely. The first thing was that she did not feel for him that fire of emotion which he felt for her; and he knew, also, that she never could love him even if he had a thousand days and the eloquence of a poet for the wooing of her. The second thing he knew was that she had determined long before to sacrifice herself to make her mother's happiness.

With a torment in his heart, but with an unreadable face, he looked back to the dying woman who was leading her daughter on to an unchangeable destiny; to satisfy a romantic whim she was sacrificing the very heart of Jacqueline. Yet it could not be called selfishness. It was rather a sublime unconsciousness of the facts of the world.

"Jacqueline!" she whispered.

"Yes!" murmured the girl, and kneeled beside the bed.

The eye of Mrs. Stoddard did not turn to her daughter, but remained lost in the tracery upon the ceiling where the shadow of a vine from the window trailed across the snowy plaster. Then she raised her hand and touched the face of the girl lightly, like that indescribable gesture with which the blind read an expression.

"You are not happy, Jack, dear," she said.

"Happiness will come later. I am willing to do what you wish," said the girl.

"Happiness will come later," said the mother.

"God bless you, dear. It means more to me than any of you can dream."

She turned her head slowly, and that slowness gave Jacqueline time to bring to her lips a smile so true and so delicately wistful that the heart of the doctor leaped in him.

To possess this fragrant and rare creature by title of law, but not in deeper truth; to have her within touch of his eyes as he pleased, though her spirit remained beyond him and strange to him; this would be a deathless pleasure. And if there was a sting of longing, yet that very unhappiness would serve to make her eternally loved and lovable in his mind. He told himself, what was indeed true, that a thing which he truly possessed he could no longer care for so deeply; the true delight was in pursuit and not in the capture.

Mrs. Stoddard was dwelling fondly on her daughter's smile now.

"Clinton and Jacqueline," she said, "take one another's hands."

The doctor made a stride nearer. His great

shadow fell black across their faces; then he kneeled beside the girl, took her passive hand in his, and felt the cold and frail fingers of the mother flutter down upon his own.

"Oh, my dears, my dears," she whispered, "do you both know what this means?"

"Yes," said the doctor, and his heart was in his throat waiting for the answer of the girl.

It came at last, a little strained and faint.

"It is a holier thing to me," she said, "than any wedding or any wedding ring, mother."

Mrs. Stoddard drew a great breath.

"Shall I tell you what it means to me? It means that I shall die happy. So happy, my dears. I have lived with a good man and a true man, dear John, and God knows I have loved him!"

Her voice swelled with emotion.

"Hush, Mary," whispered the rancher, and his voice trembled.

"And yet one part of me has stayed true to that other first love of mine, and that was your father, Clinton! John knows and understands. It has made no shadow between us, I pray."

The doctor stole a lightning glance at the face of the honest rancher. And all that he saw there was the purest pity and worship unstained with any blighting envy.

Perhaps he, too, close to the soil as he was,

had been made to love this woman all his life by the knowledge that all of her was not his. The doctor saw all of this in the split part of a second, for his brain was racing.

"No shadow, Mary," said her husband.

"And when I die," said Mary, "I shall close my eyes on this world, knowing that the one regret I had in it is brushed away. If ever ghosts come back to walk this earth, my happy spirit must come back to watch over your household, Jack and Clinton! God bless you both. But if I am wrong—if happiness does *not* come to you out of this, Jacqueline— oh, I shall come back as a wretched, wretched lost soul."

"Dear mother!" sobbed the girl. "Nothing you do can be wrong. Nothing—nothing."

It was rather a prayer than a real belief, and her hand trembled in the clasp of the doctor. He felt it, and understood, but his resolution did not falter. He pitied her, he saw her tragedy, and yet he could not give way in his purpose. Not a scruple—not an inch. He would have her or die for it.

The harsh, nasal voice of the rancher broke in. He had delayed his great news as long as possible. Now it burst from him in a flood.

"There'll be no unhappiness when she marries the doctor," he declared. "Jack loves a hard fighter and a gent with cool nerve, and the doctor is the best I ever seen. This very afternoon I've seen him walk right up to Big Jim!"

"Oh!" gasped out the mother faintly.

"No more of it," warned the doctor, rising and leaning over the invalid.

"It'll do her good," said the rancher, rejoicing as he remembered. "And—don't be so darned modest about it, son. I say that I seen Clinton walk right up to Big Jim, give him all the best of the breaks—hit him in the face, and then pull out a gun, beat Jim to the draw, and drop him in his tracks."

There was a faint moan from Mary Stoddard. Then her eyes looked up to the ceiling with a dull and steady glance. Stoddard did not dream what had happened, and even Jacqueline did not understand what that still and mysterious smile on the lips of the invalid meant, but the doctor knew at once.

It seemed strange to him that the very telling of his deed of that day should have taken a life. The bullet which had only knocked down the big gun fighter had killed Mary Stoddard.

CHAPTER TWELVE

BIG JIM'S PARTNER

"Or," said Buck, "me being a gent that's passed over his palmy days and ain't so active as I once used to be, I'd pay a dollar to him that'll nab my hoss for me."

The cow-punchers looked to one another and smiled. Had the hair of Buck been but a trifle less white they would have laughed at him to his face.

"A dollar, did you say?" grinningly replied one, and then yawned out some of the midday languor which lies heaviest upon one when the sun is hot and the lunch has been heavy.

"A dollar," repeated old Buck.

He rolled a cigarette, so that the interval would give them a chance to finish their exchange of glances and grins.

"I don't mind saying that I could use a dollar," said the big puncher who had spoken first. "And I don't mind saying that I'll earn it by roping your hoss for you—and saddling him, too, into the bargain!"

He rose to his feet. But half a dozen voices chorused a protest. Every one of them had the same desire.

"I done the first speaking," he said in defense.

"You didn't do the first thinking, though," said several of the others. "We'll toss a coin for this here party."

So a coin was tossed enough times to eliminate the unlucky, and the chosen man stood forth. He was not past thirty-five, but twenty winters and twenty summers upon the range as a full-pay puncher had made him seem older than his years. He took his rope and sauntered toward the corrals, singing out: "Lead me to this here bronc, will you?"

"He ain't hard to see," said Buck, puffing at his cigarette as though it were a cigar. "He ain't no-ways hard to make out. It's that little runt of a gray over yonder in that little corral by himself."

For it was there that he had put his mount when he dismounted and unsaddled during the lunch hour at this ranch which he had so adventitiously reached. The gray horse was a long-eared, short-legged mustang with a ewe neck and a heavy head. He had little, bright eyes winking mischievously beneath a great forelock which tumbled down like a bit of brush halfway down his forehead. And having finished the allotted portion of his hay, he stood now with a hood hoof resting upon its toe and the hip above sagging as though there were no bones in it, his lower lip dropping down, his long ears back, as though held in that place by their excessive length and weight.

"All right," said the cow-puncher, vaulting the corral fence, "and here's your hoss for you!"

As he spoke, with his head turned from the gray, or apparently turned, he made his cast, and then jerked the rope back to tighten the noose around the neck of the gray. But the noose came back like a whiplash. "Shorty" had missed, and there was a roar of laughter from the others.

As a matter of fact, the gray horse had taken one leisurely step as the rope shot through the air, so that the edge of the noose slapped him ineffectually upon the shoulder and withers. Now he stood exactly as before, except that his pendant lower lip was twitching, and that there was a spark in his eyes.

"The little rat!" cried Shorty. "Dog-goned if he didn't trick me. But I'll nail him this time!"

He began to shake out his noose once more, but there was a great voice of protest.

"You ain't got all day to make that measly dollar," said Lank Harris. "Time for a *good* man to take a try. If I miss the first shot, one of the rest of you has got a warm welcome to take my place in the corral."

Shorty hesitated. On the one hand he yearned to put his rope on the gray, quite aside from the matter of the dollar; on the other hand, the temper of Lank was not one to be tampered with, and the whole crowd was manifestly behind him. So Shorty climbed to the top rail and sat down to watch.

"You ain't got a chance," he told Lank with a sneer. "That old devil is a tricky one. Knows more in a minute about what a rope'll do than you know in a year, old son."

Lank shrugged his lean shoulders as he vaulted the fence.

Nevertheless he did not see fit to overlook the warning. He prepared his noose with care and advanced upon the gray. The latter now canted one ear forward and jogged to a farther corner. There he turned about and presented his head to the cow-puncher.

"Now's your chance," yelled the chorus, advancing toward the fence.

"Hey!" yelled Lank, swinging the end of the rope.

The pony leaped in the opposite direction, which was exactly what Lank wanted. From his right hand shot the noose, opening as it flew, and driving as straight as an arrow and almost as fast. A man could hardly have dodged that throw. But a horse has four legs with which to brace himself while a man has only two. Every one of the gray gelding's hoofs dug into the soft dirt. He stopped as though he had struck a wall; the noose into which it was intended that he should gallop fanned the tip of one ear as it fell, and the gray dropped as of old into his posture of rest.

With a great oath Lank jumped to the top of the fence, and the next puncher advanced to try his luck. But it was plain, now, that the innocent old prospector had tricked them. He had loosed them against a clever old rope-wise campaigner.

The third man tried swift movements. He advanced with a rush, feinted with the rope coil in his left hand, and when the gray horse darted to the other side, he feinted again with his right hand and the noose in it. But the gelding did not stop. It was as though he read the intention of the puncher. He plunged straight ahead, and when the cast was made, it fell much too late and merely rapped the back of his neck.

The fourth man had no better luck, and the fifth, a new hand without great skill, resigned his turn to the boss, the old puncher who was executive head of the ranch when the owner was away.

The latter entered with much ceremony, as

befitted one upon whose shoulders the honor of the outfit depended. He hitched up his sagging trousers, spat upon both hands, jerked his hat more firmly upon his head, and climbed deliberately across the fence, apostrophizing the horse as he went.

"You old son of Satan, you ornery, four-legged imp of deviltry, you old snaky-hearted man-killer, I know you and all your brothers. And when you meet me you meet your finish. I'm tougher and meaner and crookeder than you. I can rope you and ride you three times a day. I'm a heart buster, son, and you write it down in red for a fact."

As he concluded this pleasant address, he shook out his noose and began to stalk the gray, but the latter either had been excited by the former attempts or else, in the manner of the new enemy, he read a greater danger. For now he shook off his sleepiness. With both ears pricked, and with shining eyes he watched the coming of the foreman, dancing away to a safer distance continually.

Five minutes, ten minutes the foreman continued his monologue and remained slowly pursuing. Then, having lodged the gray in the narrowest corner, he came slowly down toward the horse, with both hands extended at full arm's length and a coil of rope depending from either. No horse, no matter how brilliant, could tell which was the sham and which was the noose.

The gray gelding, snorting and shaking his head, retreated until his rump was against the boards. Then, desperately he made his move. But it was not to either side. With his ears flattened, with his mouth gaped wide and lined with murderous long, yellow teeth, he rushed straight at the foreman.

There was a wild yell from the latter. He threw the rope from him and sprinted for the fence, shrieking to his men to kill the man-killer, but the cow-punchers were consumed with a passion of laughter. The dignity of their boss could never be quite the same after this day. They saw him leap for the fence; they saw him spread-eagle over the top bar and crash down on the farthest side.

He rose to his feet, spitting out dust and oaths, and his Colt in his hand. A horse like that, he told Buck fiercely, should not be allowed to live. He was a menace. Besides, Buck himself needed a disciplining for turning loose such a cagey old fighter.

Buck cut into the heart of the speech by picking up his saddle and bridle and dragging them to the corral.

"If none of you gents want that dollar," he said, "I guess that I got to take my chances." Here he took down the bars.

"If that hoss gets loose," he was warned, "you'll never in nation catch him ag'in."

"Thanks," said the miner to the good advice. "Come here, Lew, you old rascal. The game is plumb over, and there ain't going to no more fun to-day."

The gray gelding regarded his master for a dubious moment, then shook his head and walked straight to the waiting bridle. There was a yell of surprise and delight from the cowpunchers. This, then, was the dragon from which their foreman had fled!

As for the foreman, he rubbed his chin in horror. He saw his reputation shrunk to a mere rag. For there was Lew, standing downheaded as of yore and letting his master saddle him, only grunting as the cinches bit into his belly, new-stuffed with food.

"I want to ask you boys one thing," said Buck, as he climbed on the horse.

"We'll do the asking, and you can do the telling from now on," they declared.

"Is there a gent named Stoddard around these parts?"

"Drop south over them hills," they told him. "There ain't nothing *but* Stoddard over there. Take that road. It leads right past his house and on to town."

He waited for no more, but rode off into the heat of the afternoon. For two hours those tantalizingly distinct hills refused to grow any closer, and it was almost sunset before he climbed to the top of them and looked down on the great plain below.

He could see the town. But it was still miles away, and perhaps, after all, Conover was not there. It was a welcome sight to see a rider drifting up the trail toward him.

"Howdy," he called as they approached within speaking distance. And when he came closer, he halted Lew. The stranger accordingly drew rein beside him.

"I been aching for a smoke," said Buck, "but dog-goned if I didn't ride off without the makings this morning. You couldn't favor me, stranger?"

The stranger could, and rolled one for himself when Buck had finished with the makings. They twisted about in their saddles and chatted for an instant.

"You been drifting a long ways?" asked the stranger.

"Far enough to git my old hoss tired. He ain't like the hoss that I seen yesterday. Seen a big chestnut, partner, that looked like he could keep running till he dropped over the edge of the world. Except that he had a mighty big man on top of him. Never seen such a hoss."

"That so? Where was he heading?"

"Right down for these parts."

"Why, the devil, man!" cried the stranger. "You ain't meaning Big Jim?"

That was a likely enough name for Jim Conover, it seemed to Buck. "I guess that's him," he said. "Has he come through town?"

"He come *into* town," said the stranger pointedly. "But he didn't get through."

"What's that?"

"He was nicked by a tenderfoot, and he's lying dead, they say, over in town this minute!"

"Dead," cried Buck. "Dead?" And with that he spurred furiously down the road.

"He was stringing me," said the stranger darkly. "Maybe that was one of Big Jim's crooked pals."

CHAPTER THIRTEEN

A GUN FIGHTER'S FRIEND

It was after the truth was known and the spirit of Jacqueline was beginning to erect itself once more since the blow had fallen; it was after the first wild bursting of tears, when it seemed that there was no purpose in living on, since her mother was dead.

Now as she sat alone in her room, to which she had fled to mourn, and to escape from the stricken face of her father, a double torture worked in her. First she realized that she was left without her mother; and second that she was now bound by a tie of inescapable holiness to marry a man whom she did not love and whom she never could love.

Little by little, the dread of the doctor came into her mind and closed out more and more of her sorrow for her mother.

How she could marry him she could not imagine. But how she could avoid it was even more impossible to conceive.

Then another thought came to her, which was a picture of Big Jim, lying where he had fallen, in a town filled with enemies. The gun fighter lay dying while the town got drunk in honor of his fall. And she remembered him as he had been when he walked with her across the hills, big, smiling, composed, handsome, and formidable as a giant.

How many and many a time she had thought of that fellow since, and every time with a pang of regret for the manner in which she had left him. It seemed that the bullet which she had cut down the big man and which had made the doctor her future husband, had also given her a new tie with Big Jim Morne.

She went to the window. Outside it the hills were darkening. She had been hours in her room. She looked at herself in the mirror and saw that she was changed indeed. Down the hall past her room went a slow footfall, the step of her father. It paused, a door opened and shut. He had gone back to the room where her mother lay.

But what of Big Jim? Who came to him where he lay? The picture haunted her. She went out to the stables, had the groom catch her favorite pony in the corral and saddled it. Then she rode out and turned toward the town.

It was night when she entered the village. The lights from open doors and from the windows made yellow slashes and rough squares upon the white dust of the street. Yonder a dog was barking; and nearer at hand there were shrill voices of children playing and arguing in their game.

All the familiar sounds went on, and the world wagged along its way in spite of the dead woman and the man who might be dying. She had been good, and he had been strong, but their passing made no difference. It was a new thought, and a terrible one to Jacqueline.

She reached the hotel. There was quite a crowd in front of it, gathered around the hitching rack, and, rising in the stirrups, she saw the center of attraction. It was a magnificent chestnut stallion, not far from seventeen hands in height, muscled with gigantic strength, and yet with the clean and racy lines of a thoroughbred.

"Rusty is what he calls the hoss," she heard one of the men say.

It was an appropriate name. His coat was the rich red of new rust before time had browned it. But who owned it?

"Big Jim will be using his spurs when he rides that hoss ag'in," said another, "and the way he'll be riding will be straight for the tenderfoot."

It was the horse of Big Jim, then, and he was neither dead nor dying.

"You're wrong, old son," said an older man. "There ain't going to be no more trouble with Big Jim. I know his kind. He's growed to be a man, and never been beat. And this here first beating will be his last. It'll take the heart out of him.

"There he sets over in Charlie Murphy's shed, just settin' and thinkin', and no man dares go near him. But when he comes out into the light of the day again, he'll be a smaller gent in his own eyes and in the eyes of every one else, maybe."

There was a nod and a grunt from one of the bystanders. But here an urchin, fumbling at the reins of Rusty, knotted about the pole of the hitching rack, untied them. They swung back and struck against the knees of the stallion. With a snort he reared away from the gangling and snaky menace. There was a yell behind him as the crowd scattered from the neighborhood of his heels. He veered away.

"Catch him!" cried Jacqueline.

But no one else had the same idea. They shrank away as though he were his master, the gun fighter. Only one cow-puncher, fighting the big stallion away, struck him heavily across the face with a quirt which he happened to be holding in his hand. And Rusty, spurred away with the pain, rushed down the street, neighing wildly.

"There'll be the devil popping for you, kid," said some one, "when Big Jim finds out what you've done. Who'll catch the hoss up?"

But who could have caught him? He was away like a comet. Already he was out of the town.

"Maybe," said another, "Big Jim'll need a slower hoss, anyways, when he gets out of this here mess that he's in."

"When he comes out of Murphy's shed, he'll come with a gun in each hand," said another.

She waited to hear no more. Yet she was

gritting her teeth when she rode away. They had stripped Big Jim of his fame as a fighting man. They had stolen his horse away on the same day. And the bitter injustice of it, for some reason or other, called into her mind once more the face of the doctor, smiling, complacent, with a sneer not far behind the smile.

When she pulled up her pony in front of the shed behind Charlie Murphy's house, she recalled herself with a start to the fact that she did not know why she had come there. There was no helpless man for her to succor. There was only a gloomy recluse brooding over the most proper means of revenge.

Yet something made her dismount, throw the reins, and advance to the door. She unlatched it, and it swung wide of its own weight, creaking upon the rusted hinges. Out of the solid blackness of the interior came a great voice, vaguely familiar to her:

"Who the devil are you? What d'you want?"

"It's I," said Jacqueline, when she could speak. "It is only I, Jacqueline Stoddard."

There was no response for an instant, and then:

"What are you doing here?"

She trained her eyes into the darkness. The frightened beating of her heart was telling her to flee at once, while she was still safe. But she could not run away. A sort of nightmare fascination held her. And then she made out a dimly outlined, bulky figure in the center of the shop, seated, perhaps, on a barley bin or an old box.

"I thought," she said, "that you might need some help."

"Help?" cried Big Jim. "Have I got so low that I need the help of a woman?"

He added with a sudden ferocity: "You've come to see me, me being down. You've come to look me over and go back to tell the story to your friends!"

She felt her way blindly into the darkness.

"Go out," he commanded. "Go back to your father and the sneaking skunk of a tenderfoot that he brung along with him. Tell them that I'm coming for 'em both. Tell 'em that. I'll be there right at your heels."

She did not stir a step backward. Instead, she went straight on until she was close before him.

"There was something that brought me in," she said simply, "and now I see what it is. It is to tell you that you mustn't go near Doctor Aylard."

The man in the dark laughed. "I'm to swaller what he's done?" he suggested ironically.

115

"Oh," said the girl, "don't you see what it means? If you fight him again, even if you win, you lose. Other men will try what he tried. You sign your own death warrant if you use your guns again, Big Jim."

"Did they send you in here?"

"No."

"What brought you?"

"I remembered a kind thing which you once did for me, Big Jim."

"Oh?" said he.

"And I've come to apologize for the last thing I said to you that day. You've forgotten it, but I never have."

There was a long moment of pause.

"I'm sure dreaming this," said he. "This ain't the truth—it can't be. In your mind, I'm wrote down a snake."

"No, no!"

"Will you gimme your hand on that, Jacqueline?"

She fumbled, found his hand, and noted how tenderly it closed over her own.

"Now," said he, as he released her, "I believe you. It's the first time that a man or a woman in these parts has made me feel that I was trusted. Heaven knows what put it into your head that I ain't a plain, no-good man-killer. But what else is there left for me? Can you tell me that? If I take water from Aylard

116

this way, the Chinamen will be laughing at me, let alone the self-respecting cow-punchers."

"And what if you meet him and beat him?"

"Then I'm back where I started. Back where I was before to-day."

"And where was that, Big Jim?"

There was another long pause.

"Heaven knows," he said at last. "Nothing pretty about it, I know well enough. But I'm fixed in a corner where there's nothing left to me but guns to fight my way out. What else could I do and save my honor?"

"Do nothing except to live quietly, like an honest man."

"And be laughed at?"

"Do you care what they think?"

"No, darn 'em, I despise the whole lot!"

"Then live as if you despised *them,* but not *yourself.*"

"In this range? Where there's not a friend for me?"

"There's one, Big Jim."

"And who?"

"You've shaken hands with her to-night."

CHAPTER FOURTEEN

A RESCUE PARTY

The news came to the House of Morne, borne by a rider whose horse dripped foam from neck and belly when it was reined in. That very morning they had swelled big with their pride in their old champion returned to them; but the hard rider carried them word that Big Jim was down at last, and down before the gun of a tenderfoot. And every man and woman and child in the hollow was convulsed with rage and with shame and with fear.

Old John Morne himself was sitting under the tree before his house when the news came. It bowed him over until he was forced to support his chin on both of his hands. He remained there for a long time. When he raised his head it was to order the young men to saddle their horses and take their guns; and to prepare the buckboard for him.

So the old buckboard was rolled out. To it a pair of the finest horses were hitched, and the reins were placed in the hands of the veteran leader.

The youngsters made their own horses

ready, and in a moment the work was done. They flashed into the corrals, darted their ropes out, caught the first wild-eyed pony that came within range, and snapped a saddle upon its back. Then they plunged back to stand ready around John Morne.

The old man looked them over with an eye in which pride and contempt were equally mingled. They were fearless, and every one willing to accept the word of John Morne as if it were freshly transcribed from the Bible. But they made wretched substitutes for the lost men who had once ridden behind him.

The youngest of them was a scant fourteen; the eldest was barely seventeen. In truth, they were children in all things except what their wild life with horses and guns and rubbing elbows with crime had given to them. Their virtues were the virtues of wild beasts; their vices were much the same. They were as brave, as cunning, as ferocious as young panthers; but they were also as treacherous, as fickle, as cruel. They needed to be led. There was nothing that could be asked of them that they would not grant if it came to bloodshed, for everyone of them had been raised to consider that the rest of the world was banded against the Pattisons and the Mornes, and therefore it was the bounden duty of Pattisons and Mornes to strike back against a cruel and aggressive world.

They were dressed in rags. The hair blew long and wild about their faces; that long hair they particularly affected, which was a sort of a badge of their clan. Their upper lips were shaven clean, but no razor touched their chins; and beards were beginning to darken upon their faces, giving them an almost foolish mask of age.

As for their equipment, the horses were lean, humpbacked mustangs. That breed had grown scarce among the ranchers of that range. They bred for themselves a finer and a sleeker stock. But the invincible savagery and wiry endurance of the mustang could not be replaced. John Morne had reestablished that race for the use of himself and his clan. And the horses they rode were as wild, as unkempt as the men themselves.

Each man wore, in a case under his left leg, the rifle upon which he was taught chiefly to depend in all times of trouble.

"It's a pile better," John Morne had said to them a thousand times, "that you should shoot once and shoot straight, than shoot twenty times and miss or just nick a man."

So all the Mornes and the Pattisons used rifles and shot straight indeed. There were four Mornes and three Pattisons who reined their horses before their leader in the buckboard this evening. Each had a pair of revolvers, also, heavy ammunition belts, and at least one formidable knife apiece.

But that was far from the least of their training. Old John Morne himself was famous with the cold steel, and he taught his clan to whip a heavy knife out of the palm of the hand, driving it so forcefully with a mere twist of the wrist that the blade became a glint of light and was driven half its length into the tree trunk at which it was flung.

With knives, revolvers, rifles, every boy and man in the clan practiced each day of his life. The poorest performer was forced to do the lion's share of the chores, and therefore the poorest performer of one day became, by assiduous training, the best of another day.

They could all ride any horse they could bestride. They had lived in the mountains, on the deserts, until their eyes were animal bright with the wisdom of the trail. They could almost tell by the manner of the buzzards as they circled up the wind and then dropped from sight what sort of a prey they had found. They could almost read the scents upon the wind. While every one, even the youngest, could take rifle and salt and cross the desert on foot, finding food and water in plenty where others starved at once.

Indeed, the test of manhood in the clan was

not age or even skill with weapons, but the ability to go from the ranch, with only that small pouch of salt and with the rifle and the ammunition, and cross the desert in the full terror of the mid-summer sun, passing to a blue mountaintop a hundred miles away, and returning, all within the space of five days. This meant forty miles a day for five days under a terrible sun and through the desert sands which flow and melt away beneath the step.

There was an unfailing proof that the journey had been made, and this was to come back with a pocketful of purple red haws—the kind which grew upon no other mountainside in the whole vicinity. The haws were the proof, and they could not be imitated. Yet this tremendous journey had been made in turn by each of the party.

The youngest, who was barely fourteen years old, had performed the feat not five days before, and his face was still thin and savagely hard from the agony through which he passed. He had collapsed when he returned to the hollow, and had lain, unable to move, for hours. But the reward was worth the torment, in his eyes, for he had the glorious distinction of being the youngest Morne who was ever acclaimed a "man."

In other ways, too, he was worthy of his

place among the seven young wild men. His stubborn wrists had learned to manage the weight of a Colt forty-five of the standard model; but his rifle was only a thirty-two, with a short barrel. Other than this he could ride and shoot with the best of them.

In the opinion of the whole Morne clan, young Don Pattison, for that was his name, would one day be a great man—almost as great, perhaps, as Big Jim himself.

Yet John Morne, as he looked over the four young heroes of his own name and the three who bore the name of Pattison, smiled grimly. Another year or two and they would have hardened into true maturity.

Jerry Morne, already prematurely cunning, would be eighteen and capable of leading as well as any man. But in the meantime, to expose them too soon to the evils of the world, would be to blight their growth and their promise. Another short year and he would be surrounded by seven young giants. Alas, that big Jim was not to take them into his protection until they should no longer need it!

These were the thoughts which ran through the brain of the old leader, but what he said was to express another thought which was also in him.

"Men," said John Morne, and at that word the youngsters stiffened in their saddles, "men, you've heard how Big Jim has gone down. What they've done to him by this time, Heaven knows. Mostlike, after he dropped, they took him out and lynched him. If they did, we'll have blood for his blood. If they didn't, we'll bring him back safe and sound to the hollow. We're riding straight into town to get him."

There was a sound in response. For the town had been the one place where the Mornes had not roved. It was the stronghold of the enemy, and to enter that town in procession, armed to the teeth, would be inviting trouble.

John Morne knew it even better than the rest, but he also knew that since the great blow had fallen it was necessary to do some striking thing to show that his power was not extinct.

He did not wait for an answer. He spoke to the team, bracing his one foot against the dashboard, and as the horses plunged away, the whole group of youngsters followed him with a yell.

When night covered the town, the Mornes arrived in it. The news of their coming flew ahead of them as if carried by arrows. They paused on the outskirts of the town to find out what had become of Big Jim, and as they learned they gave time for the news of their arrival to spread.

It caused the men of the place to gather at the hotel to await a cause for action under the direction of the sheriff. And there it was that Buck, newly arrived, heard of their coming and of the place where Big Jim was sitting by himself. He went like the wind, reached the open door of the shed of Charlie Murphy, and threw himself from his horse.

"Conover!" he called.

"Buck!" cried the voice of Big Jim.

And, in another instant, they had clasped hands.

"Your friends, the Mornes, are coming, hell bent, for you, Jim!"

"Don't wait for them, Jim," said a girl's voice in the darkness, and Buck made her out dimly for the first time, "If you go back with them, it's the beginning of the end."

"You're right, Jack," said Conover. "Now's the time for me to break away. I'll get my hoss."

"Rusty broke away from the rack. You won't find him there."

A groan from Conover answered her.

"Did the hounds steal Rusty away from me while I was down?"

"It was an accident—" she began.

He stopped her with a growl. "It's too much, Jack. They've badgered me and cornered me, and I go back with the Mornes.

There ain't nothing else left for me to do."

He stood up, looking gigantic in the darkness. "Go now, Jack. God bless you for coming. But it ain't any use. I'm too old to change. There's too many agin' me. They've stole my hoss and my honor. Ride away before any one knows that you've been here with me."

There was a sob from the girl, then the swishing of her skirt as she hurried to the door, and the rattling hoofs of her horse as she rode away.

"So," said Conover heavily, "there's the end of that."

"What's it mean?" queried Buck.

"It means that I go back with the Mornes— that a regular war starts, mostlike, and that we all get wiped out. But there ain't anything left for me to do; they've cornered me. Go back to the mine, Buck. My share of it is yours."

Conover turned away.

"Why," said Buck, "I'm tired of mining. If there's trouble ahead, and you're mixed up in it, here's where I stay, old-timer!"

CHAPTER FIFTEEN

STRANGE PROCEEDINGS

What promised to be a tragedy passed off with perfect smoothness. The men of the town waited near the hotel for the first sound of a rifle shot. Then they were prepared to wipe out the Mornes, root and branch. But there was not the sound of a gun.

The Mornes found Big Jim, placed him in the buckboard at the side of old Morne, and they rode back to the hollow, yelling and whooping their triumph.

There were some men who accused the sheriff of slackness in allowing the famous gun fighter to be taken safely out of the town and back to his clan where he would be a tower of strength against all law-abiding citizens. But the sheriff silenced all those who complained.

"There's plenty of old counts agin' Big Jim that he could be arrested on," he said, "but we didn't figure that there was any of 'em worth using before he was downed by the doctor. And we ain't going to jump on him now that he's down. As for the whole Morne gang, the first time that one of 'em starts a fight, I'm going to take enough men down to wipe up the whole lot of 'em. But we'll wait for that time. Understand?"

And there was something so eminently fair, such good sportsmanship in this attitude, that the whole town had to admit that the sheriff was right, as usual.

In the meantime, old Buck rode back with the young Mornes, while Big Jim and the cripple journeyed in the buckboard.

Old John was highly elated.

"We've showed 'em what we're made of," he declared. "We've cleaned 'em up, and be darned to 'em all. We've rode right into the middle of the town and got you away from 'em. And now, Jim, you'll stay with us?"

"Where else can I stay?" said Jim.

"Keep the boys together for one year," said old John, "and then you're welcome to go where you like."

"How can I keep 'em together?" asked Big Jim.

"I dunno. But I know that if they wander around, they'll get into fights, and the first fight will be the last one for all of us. If a Morne pulls a gun on any man, no matter how much he's in the right, there'll be hell popping. The sheriff will come down on us with an army, mostlike!"

"You want me to keep 'em close to the hollow

for a year?"

"Yep."

"What'll they live on in the meantime?"

"I dunno," said John Morne.

"What *have* they been livin' on?"

"There's been pickings."

"You mean that when crooks come through they lay up with you and pay you pretty handsome for their board?"

"Maybe that's the one way of getting a little money."

"And another way is supplying men to every long rider that comes through and needs a gang for some work?"

"That's been done, Jim. We got to live, don't we?"

"But now all that riding has got to stop?"

"It sure does!"

Big Jim made no further comments. He was too full of thought for more words. It was not the problem of the Mornes alone that troubled him. There was the question of his own affairs, and never had they seemed so strange or complex to him.

To revenge himself on the doctor had been the first impulse, for something told him that the courage of Aylard had sprung out of his medical knowledge. Everything was explained the instant Big Jim knew that the tenderfoot was a physician.

His trained eye had recognized the malady of Conover. He knew that the revolver which Jim wore upon his right hip was indeed no better than a wooden gun, and therefore he had attacked a practically helpless man and come close to murder.

Jim Conover touched the bandage around his aching head and ground his teeth. If the bullet had flown a fraction of an inch lower, it would have passed through his brain. And looking the whole matter over, he knew that he had never yet heard of so dastardly an action in his life. The real irony of fate was that the doctor would be made a hero by the people on account of his very cowardice.

So much for the doctor. And something told him that if he put his gun upon his left hip and fought Aylard with the weapon in his left hand, he would dispose of the tenderfoot as easily as the tenderfoot had disposed of him. Now his position was vastly complicated. If he removed the protection of his name and fame, even though it had lately dwindled, from the Mornes, their enemies would butcher them like dogs. And if he went to hunt down the doctor, that killing would also be a signal for the countryside to rise against the men of the hollow.

For both these reasons he must stay quietly in the hollow. For he could not give up these foster people. He had been touched to the very heart by the instant courage with which they had come to his rescue in the town. If they were willing to risk their lives for him he must do the same for them.

Yet there was another angle. If he stayed with the Mornes, he lost Jacqueline, and the very softness and quality of her voice was still at his ear, as she had told him her faith in him to become an honest man.

It had been the sweetest of music to Conover. He felt now as though he would pay with a year of life for ten more words from her. But he had given up that hope by coming back with the Mornes. She could never know him while he dwelt among such people. But if he left them—who could tell? In the darkness of that room, there had been something between them. It had flown like electricity, and strange, wild hopes had begun to grow up in his mind.

All that was ended, and he had put to death those hopes by coming back with John Morne and the others. He could never see Jacqueline again, or if he saw her, the old scorn and hatred would be in her face as it had been on that day five years before when she left him.

It was a melancholy man who reached the hollow. He was given a room in the shack of John Morne himself. He was given a supper in the dining room that was a feast.

Four women of the Mornes and the widows of Mat and Oliver Pattison all tended him with tender voices and smiling lips. But when their glances touched upon the bandage which encircled his forehead, their eyes filled with flames. In his fall, something of their own pride in their race had fallen.

It seemed to Big Jim that the fawning tenderness and solicitude with which they cared for him and brought for him their best jellies, their choicest cuts of cold meets, their leanest bacon, their whitest bread, their most fragrant coffee, showed only a feline cunning. They would fatten him, strengthen him, hearten him to stand forth again and offer himself as a bulwark between their children and the danger of the world.

After the meal he nodded to John Morne, and the latter, with a gesture, banished the womenfolk. They talked for five minutes, and Big Jim learned what he wished. There were seven men, or youths who called themselves men, besides Buck and Big Jim and John Morne. There were six women, all mothers. There were eight children. Not counting John and Conover and Buck, there were twenty-one souls in the hollow.

To provide for them, there was enough food in the larders to last for three or four days.

When they ran out of that, as John Morne said with a grin, there were plenty of cows straying in the hills near by. As for hard cash, there was hardly a penny on the place.

So Big Jim sat before his window that night and did not close his eyes. He was afraid to lie down, for then the memory of Jack would come to torment his heart, and the old, wild desire to destroy Aylard would become a monomania. He remained awake and watched the stars glittering behind the tops of the lofty trees.

Out of the trees themselves he gained his first inspiration. The next morning he sallied out immediately after breakfast with a keen ax in his hand. He selected a monster of the grove and sank the blade half its length in the tender wood, so that the sap oozed up around the steel. He jerked it out and struck again, until the noise of the blows brought the children and then the young men.

In ten minutes they were all at work, and he kept them at it all the day. When they asked him questions, he shook his head and refused to answer. So they gritted their teeth as the blisters swelled and broke on the palms of their hands under this unaccustomed chafing and labor. But they worked on.

Rumors began to fly about. Big Jim intended to erect a huge palisade around the house so that they would be dwelling in a real fortress from which they could defy the rest of the world. Such talk kept them busy and contented.

Even when Old John Morne asked questions that night, Conover offered no explanation, except to say: "You've turned over this game into my hands. I'm going to play it in my own way, and I don't want no advice."

The next day he sent Buck to town.

"Find old Hughson, the banker," he said, "and get him out here. You don't have to tell him what for. Just tell him that Big Jim has a business proposition. He'll be so curious that he can't keep away."

Buck departed, and the axes continued to ring all that morning. But after lunch Jud Pattison refused to rise from his seat on a bunch of pine needles. His hands were too sore, he said, and, besides, he saw no point in work whose meaning was not explained to him.

The news of this desertion spread the rounds. The others consulted the soreness of their hands and hesitated. So Big Jim, seeing that stern measures were necessary, went over to the first recalcitrant.

"Get up, Jud," he said, without malice.

Jud swaggered to his feet.

"Pick up your ax," said Jim.

"I'll see you damned first," said the boy hotly. "How come that you're a slave driver around here? Who made you my—"

He got no further. The immense left fist of Big Jim clipped him on the base of the jaw, and he went down like a blade of grass that the scythe has touched. When he recovered, Big Jim dragged him to his feet.

"You fool," he said to Jud, "you ain't working for me. You're working for your mother and your kid brother and old John Morne and all the rest of us. You'll do your share, or I'll brain you."

Jud recovered from his frenzy. He looked around him, but he encountered no superior and mocking smiles. There was nothing but the ringing of axes as his companions fell furiously to work, and Jud mechanically picked up his own tool. In an hour he had worked away his rage, and by the time it had departed, Big Jim stood before him.

"Jud," said he, "I oughtn't to of hit you. I'm here to ask your pardon."

And it was given with a will.

That was the end of trouble, at least for the time being. That afternoon, the arrival of Hughson put an end to the mystery behind the labor. The banker came in a fever of curiosity.

"You after money?" he asked Big Jim,

135

shortly after he arrived.

"Everybody is," said Jim. "And I'm going to get it."

"What security?" said the banker sharply.

"There's enough wood in a couple of them big trees to build a house," said Conover. "What will you pay?"

"In cash?"

"In grubstakes out of your store," said Jim, looking him in the eye, "and in plows and harrows and work harness for hosses."

"What the devil," said Hughson, "are you going to be a farmer, in this here country?"

"Look yonder up the hollow," said Jim. "There's three hundred acres of trees and swamp. If there's water enough to make a swamp, there's water enough to irrigate. And all we need is to cut down the big timber and burn the small. does it sound good to you?"

Hughson removed his hat and whistled between his teeth.

CHAPTER SIXTEEN

JACK NAMES A DAY

Mrs. Stoddard had been placed in her grave. A week passed, but still Doctor Aylard found himself no nearer to the marriage than before. Of course, ordinarily he would not have expected to crowd a death and a marriage so closely together, but he felt that this occasion was far different, for the dying wish of Mrs. Stoddard had been for the union of her daughter and the doctor, and therefore the most pious action of Jacqueline would be to give her hand to Aylard, but she said nothing about it.

Her father now and again referred to the approaching ceremony, but Jacqueline always heard these remarks in silence and with an expression of pain which touched even the stony heart of the doctor; and he, for his part, remained resolutely quiet.

Perhaps it was lucky that he was little with the girl during that time, for Stoddard had taken him under his wing and was initiating him into the mysteries of ranch affairs and ranch management.

"But," the doctor used to protest, "it's a life work, learning to handle a ranch, and I know nothing of the cow business."

"It's a life work or two lives' work to learn how to handle a gun the way you handle one," said Stoddard in reply. "All you got to do is to open your mind and try. I'll feed in the facts. You just digest them."

There was nothing else for the doctor to do

for a few days, and he showed himself such an astonishingly apt pupil that Stoddard predicted a great future for him.

The doctor, for his part, never had the slightest intention of applying himself to the work; but since, as the natural heir to the place when he married Jacqueline, it was proper to understand ranch management, he threw himself with a zest into the new rôle. But in his heart of hearts he told himself that a foreman and a business manager would be his representatives on the place.

He was beginning to weaken on the subject of the sale of the property as soon as Stoddard died, however.

To be sure, the building of Aylard House in England in a proper state of glory, was still as dear to him as ever. He used to sit up long hours in his room planning the details, from the stables to the bathrooms, for he intended to harmonize old effects with modern conveniences; but in order to build such an establishment, he would have to sell the ranch and invest some of the capital at once in the new structure, and he was feeling less and less inclined to make such a move.

If he sold the ranch, it meant that he was uprooted from the West, and this thought became more and more distasteful, for in the West he was beginning to feel that he was taking his proper place in society.

After all, the Aylards had ever been a fighting family. An Aylard had struck at the Saxon wedge of shields and axes at Hastings. An Aylard had smashed Saracen skulls in the Crusades, and here in the cattle country he was prëminently respected as a fighting man.

In England he could at best expect to found a great house, a great family, and the only thing which could complete his work would be time—a couple of centuries of it. He would be a moldered and almost forgotten image by that point in time, and still, when all was said, the Alyards would be considered a comparatively new family in green England, and he, the founder, would be a mere interloper.

Of course, he told himself, it was better to be an interloper in England than a hero in the West of the States, and yet there was something infinitely soothing in the latter position. When he rode into the town, now, he was received with more heartfelt ceremony than a United States senator.

Old ranchers whose history was inextricably mixed with that of the beginnings of civilization in the mountain desert came hunting for him, to shake his hand and tell him what a great blow he had struck in behalf of peace and order in the land. Then they launched into long narratives of the exploits of famous fighters whom they themselves had known, but the doctor learned to listen and to nod, for, after all, he knew that they were secretly flattering him by comparisons.

Though on the one hand he considered them a tobacco-flavored race of barbarians, yet on the other hand, he could not help admitting that by their deeds they had proved themselves men. Above all, their flattery of him made them important.

If chance led him up the steps of the hotel, he heard from the loungers on either side a murmur as of bees; and sweeter than honey was that sound to the doctor. If he passed a buckboard on the road, he was deliciously conscious of the battery of eyes that followed him as he rode on.

The doctor, at such times, found a mist of pleasure in his eyes. He could almost have wept with the joy of it, and what made the whole affair so doubly entrancing was that he had accomplished his end by sheer bluff.

He who wins with a royal flush has enjoyed the thrilling presence of good luck and has fattened his bank account, no doubt, but he who beats down the opposition with nothing more than a pair of deuces, and beats it down by the iron of his will and the exquisite rapier point of sham, has felt himself raised to a tenth heaven. He has asserted his mental and spiritual superiority. He begins to feel in himself the ability to move mountains. It was so with the clever doctor.

He was well aware that he played a dangerous game. He was well aware that the gun he carried was only a wooden weapon of pretense. Every day he cantered off by himself and exercised his hand with revolver work, but he could not acquire in a short time the marvelous skill which belonged to old cowpunchers who had spent their lives in similar practice. He was a good shot and he learned to get out his weapon fast enough, but he had not that lightning draw and that deadly and instinctive accuracy of aim. If his bluff should ever be called, he knew that he was a gone man.

Yet the knowledge that he was living in a deadly peril increased his happiness proportionately. He was no weak-nerved gambler. He was content to make life itself one of the stakes. What he won in exchange was applause, and applause is what many men strive for. To Aylard it meant that he was being instinctively granted that little which had been stolen away from him. When these roughhanded Westerners fell silent out of respectful admiration when he entered a room, it was as if they addressed him by some title of nobility.

So the good doctor remained on the range,

happily, uneasily, watching the signs of the time to see when his sham might be penetrated by some daring cow-puncher fuller of drink than of discretion. He waited, also, for the favorable opportunity to press his suit with Jacqueline, for the time had about come when he must speak to her.

Yet the occasion of that speaking was most unfortunate. He had ridden away from the ranch house immediately after breakfast. He had headed for a small hollow with which he was familiar and in which he had tried the same sport before.

In the midst of the rock walls of the gap, where the sounds of his guns could not carry far away across the landscape, he began to cut loose, firing with either hand and from a variety of positions. Given plenty of time for his draw and for his shot, he was as excellent a marksman as one could wish to see, but it was not mere accuracy which he tried for. Speed was the thing he wanted to get, and when he tried for speed, the results were not pleasing.

His system was to place small black rocks on the top of a great white boulder. At these he blazed away, riding his horse back and forth, sometimes with his back to the targets, wheeling in the saddle and firing in haste; sometimes he galloped past them and blazed away, but his misses were ten to one against his hits.

His guns were hot and his temper sorely tried when, looking up to the edge of the gap, he saw no other than Jacqueline looking down upon him. For the moment the heart of the doctor stood still. In the first place, he had chosen to let it be known that his revolver skill did not need great practice. In the second place, if his real lack of skill were known, he was little better than a dead man. Some Morne or Pattison would instantly hunt him down.

But he had two hopes. The first was that Jacqueline, even if she had marked his lack of adroitness at that distance, would keep the secret. The second was that she had been too far off to make out his targets.

She had started to rein away her horse, when she observed that he had seen her. Then she paused for him, in answer to his shout, and he spurred up the slope to her side.

"You have found me out," said the doctor, with a laugh. "You see that I have to keep my hand in with a little work every day."

She looked him straight in the eye with the faintest of smiles, and he saw that she had indeed been able to see too much. In spite of himself, he flushed, for he could understand the wonder with which she stared at him.

Having such small skill with guns, how had he dared to attack Big Jim?

And how under heaven had he been able to conquer that great warrior?

If she should gain the clew to the mystery, if she should know that he had taken advantage of a stricken man, how utterly would she scorn him. But as it was, he felt that he had simply thrown another veil of mystery around his shoulders. He decided to speak while she was still astonished.

"Jack," he said, as he rode on at her side, "the days are running along. We're no closer to a certain thing that must be done. What do you say about it?"

He saw her lose color while her glance wandered to the sky line.

"I don't know," she said finally. "Of course, I understand what you mean, but there is something I have to tell you, Clinton."

He nodded, swallowing the lump of fear which had risen to his throat.

"What is it, Jack?"

"You know that I respect my mother's will."

"I know that."

"And if you care to marry me, I must do as she wished. But——"

He bit his lip. Then he waited.

"But if I marry you, you must know that—

144

that I really haven't yet come to—to care for you in that way. It's only fair to you to tell you that, isn't it? Because what a great unhappiness there would be ahead of you if—if this should be all a mistake!"

And as the last words burst from her, she lifted her head and looked at him with great eyes of appeal.

He understood perfectly. It was her last plea that he spare her the sacrifice, and he thanked Heaven that he had prepared the answer long before.

"I know what you mean, Jack. You've been waiting for that rosy haze of romance. It hasn't fallen on me, unfortunately, but most of these romantic marriages don't turn out so very well.

"There's your own mother and father. It was not exactly a romantic marriage, but yet it turned out very well. Certainly she loved him before the end, and I have a certainty that I can make you happy, my dear. Do you think that you could trust me enough to let me try?"

Actual persuasion could not have succeeded. He had decided on the very first day that he would simply meet appeal with appeal. Against his gentleness and sadness, he saw that she had no defense. Her head fell. She sighed.

"I have nothing more to say, if you wish it

to be that way," she said.

She might scorn him for not giving her freedom, but possession was nine points in the game, and once he possessed her with his ring, he would take a chance on what might come thereafter. He pushed ahead with his points.

"Then it's settled, Jack. It only remains for you to name a day——"

"A day?" She looked up again with a sort of despair.

"Yes."

"I don't know," she said, her voice trembling.

"I—I suppose that we had better have it done with soon——"

"By all means!" he murmured.

She glanced widely around her and then pointed toward the horizon. "Look there!" she cried. "Isn't that like a sign?"

He looked in the direction which she had indicated and he saw a great chestnut stallion with a gleaming body in the sunlight, flashing across the skyline with half a dozen mares following at his heels.

"What's that?" he cried. "Gad, what a horse!"

"It's Big Jim's stallion. It's his horse, Rusty," she answered. "And because I hate definite set dates, I'll marry you the very day

146

you catch him, Clinton!"

He watched the great horse and his band disappear over the edge of a hill. There had been talk of the chestnut in the past few days. He had rubbed off his saddle and torn off his bridle after he ran loose from the town the day of the shooting of Big Jim, and now he was careering through the mountains with a band of mares, recruited from day to day. One hour of wild freedom was worth a year of tame life. Already he had reverted to the wilderness.

No doubt it would be easy enough to capture the great animal if men enough were put on his trail. In the meantime, it was not hard to understand how poor Jacqueline, vainly seeking for a way to postpone the marriage, had hit upon this expedient.

He could have smiled at the childishness of it, but no smile came, for it seemed rather a gloomy foreboding that the shadow of Big Jim should have fallen across his path at this moment of all moments in his life!

CHAPTER SEVENTEEN

HARRISON COLBY

For Big Jim, the visit from Harrison Colby could not have come at a more inopportune time. With the passing of every day it had been increasingly difficult to keep the Mornes and the Pattisons at work.

Without the influence of the women, indeed, he would have been quite unable to succeed, but they stood by him stanchly instead in the time of need. They saw their larders filled with more and better supplies than had been in them for many a long week, and it did not much matter to them how the food came, so long as it duly arrived. The elder women were only mildly complacent; but the younger ones who had infant children and no husbands to support them in a time of disaster were the fierce champions of the new leader.

As for the youngsters who now took the place of men among the Mornes, they only knew that some sort of contract had been entered into between Big Jim and Hughson, the banker. They knew that, as a result of this contract, they received abundant food, implements for farm work, plows, harrows, harness and a hundred odds and ends. No doubt Big Jim, the gun fighter, the man-destroyer, had some mysterious goal, but in the meantime it looked very much as though he were simply turning them into farmers.

Talk began to buzz abroad. It was said that Big Jim had been unnerved by his defeat at the hands of the tenderfoot. It was said that, knowing he could not lead a wild and free life any longer, since he had been crushed in battle, he had determined to settle down to a plodding and safe existence under the shelter of the law. Of course this talk was not entirely believed, but each day's work with the axes gave it stronger plausibility.

Had the youngsters been told that he did indeed intend to make of them steady working farmers, they would not have performed an instant's more work for him; but the awe in which they held him, and the lingering hope that all of this was only an elaborate piece of maneuvering to deceive the law-abiding ranchers of the neighborhood, held them to their places.

Nevertheless, their restlessness was increasing rapidly. They went several times a day to old John Morne with questions. He was as worried and as baffled as they were, but he had to pretend knowledge. He could not, for the sake of his own dignity, let them know how completely he had been pushed into the background. So he winked and smiled and advised them that time would tell its story and that Big Jim had never played the fool yet.

With these words he turned them away, but in private he drew Big Jim aside.

"You're riding for a fall, son," he told the giant. "If you're really meaning to turn these lads into farmers, you're going to make a failure. Might as well try to turn swords into plowshares."

But Big Jim replied only with a shrug of his shoulders. In the meantime, the forest was crashing down. The heavy teams of Hughson were dragging the great logs to town. Brush was being cleared away. The face of the swamp was being laid bare.

"Places where we could all of us hide a hundred times over," the boys complained, "and Big Jim is layin' it all wide, so's any bunch of fools could hunt us down. Opening up a stinking marsh—we'll all of us have malaria out of it."

And so, begrudgingly, they continued their labors. When the trees were down, they were put at the more repulsive task of digging ditches through the slush, and erecting small dams here and there at high points.

For the first time they were able to see Morne hollow clearly. It revealed itself as part swamp, indeed, but partly wide-stretching meadows of level, immensely rich river-bottom lands.

Then Harrison Colby came.

He arrived at night, as a matter of course. Men with such a price on their heads as he carried could not be expected to expose themselves rashly to the light of day any more than if every ray of the light had been a bullet searching for their lives. When the door opened upon him, he found Big Jim and old John Morne sitting together, old John trying to extract the secret of the great work from his foster son, and Big Jim, labor-crushed, head bowed, smoking his pipe and staring at the open fire with calculating eyes.

What he was calculating was not how many feet of ditch could be dug in the swamp the next day, but what the effect of his work might be in the heart of Jacqueline Stoddard. Would she guess that he had not returned to the Mornes to be a partner of their crimes? Would she guess that he had a greater and more constructive purpose?

They turned and faced Harrison Colby. He was a tall, thin, erect man of fifty. His hair was black. His narrow beard was almost white. He had high cheek bones, sunken cheeks, great

151

bushy eyebrows, glittering black eyes. He looked like a cross between a red-handed pirate and an old cavalier. As a matter of fact, he did not belie his looks. He had committed crimes enough to have hanged a dozen men, but he could carry himself with a high manner which still served to obscure his more vital nature to chance acquaintances.

Neither Big Jim nor John Morne were chance acquaintances, however. They knew him of old, and that was the reason they greeted him without a smile, without a query as to his well-being.

"How many miles you done since sunset?" was all that Big Jim could think to ask his guest.

Colby had made himself at home beside the fire, knocking the dust off his boots, while his spurs jingled, and then lighting a long, thin, black cigar. The enjoyment of it made him close his eyes. He opened them lazily to respond.

"Thirty-five," he said. "Thirty-five miles since sunset."

"The devil!" said Big Jim.

"No one hoss carried you," said John Morne.

"Nope. I killed the first one inside fifteen miles and borrowed another out of the first corral I come to. Left him about eight miles

152

back, borrowed another, and here I am!"

They regarded him with the keenest interest. Cold-blooded devil though he was, he was nine parts of a hero, also. Any man who could ride thirty-five miles in such a space of time without being exhausted was worthy of whole-hearted admiration.

"That's something," remarked Big Jim," that I never done. I never killed a hoss."

"That's something worth doing that's still before you, Conover," said the outlaw, and smiled evilly.

Big Jim started, and Morne bellowed: "What name did you call him?"

"I know new names and old uns too," grinned Colby. "But let it rest. I got a deal on to-night. How many you got here to ride with me, John?"

Morne straightened in his chair. "The old boys are gone," he said, "but there's some youngsters with us that ain't to be sneezed at, Colby."

The outlaw nodded. "A Morne at ten years is worth most other men at thirty," he said calmly. "I guess Big Jim ain't ready to ride with me?"

"I want none of your game," said Conover coldly, "and I never did want any of it."

"Steady, boys, steady!" broke in Morne in the greatest anxiety, for the two were glaring at each other with eyes of fire.

Colby controlled himself and turned his head to Morne, though his glance was still malevolently fastened upon the face of the big man.

"I say, how many of your kids can I have?"

"How many do you want?"

"Three handy lads will do."

"You sure can have——"

"Wait a minute," said Big Jim. "I'll answer them questions."

"What?" cried Colby. "Are *you* the boss here now?"

"I am."

Colby rose from his chair and crossed to the door. "I got into the wrong church," he sneered. "I'll be going along."

"Wait a minute, Colby," panted Morne. "Jim, d'you see what you're doing?"

"I see it all plumb easy and clear. What of it?"

"I say that more money has been made through Colby for us than through all the rest of 'em."

"Can you deny that, Big Jim?" snapped Colby. "Ever knowed me to try my hand at any small deal? Ever knowed me to fail? Ever knowed me to split any ways but square with all my partners in any game?"

Jim hesitated. "Suppose I call in the boys

and let 'em hear your proposition?" he suggested at last.

Colby bit his lip while he considered; but since he was unable to see that there was any trap in this suggestion, he nodded amiably enough.

"Bring 'em in," he said. "That's just what I want. I want 'em to hear what I got to offer."

Big Jim walked to the wall and took down an old horn. Then, from the door, he blew in a deep and moaning blast. It was the meal signal in the day. It was the rallying call for the men by night.

He had hardly hung up the horn again and returned to his place beside the fire, before the youngsters began to pour into the doorway, half dressed, their eyes glittering with excitement, their weapons shining in their hands.

A jubilant young army!

"Like a nest of young catamounts," grinned Colby, as he looked over the array. "Morne, you sure do raise 'em rough."

The old man expanded with the compliment.

"Boys," said Big Jim, waving toward Colby, "I guess that the most of you have heard a good deal about Harrison Colby. But some of you ain't been quite old enough to see him yet. There he is. He's going to tell you one side of a proposition. Then I'm going to tell you another side of it. When we both are through, we'll make up our minds about what we want to do for him."

CHAPTER EIGHTEEN

THE TEMPTATION

There was no doubt that every boy there knew all about Harrison Colby's exploits. Their eyes shone with a new fire. It was like showing a famous scalp taker to a group of young Indians who have yet to step on their first warpath.

Colby drank in their excitement, running his eye carefully over their faces. It was patent that he had the battle more than half won, even before he spoke a word.

"It's a game that I could pull off all by myself," he told them, "but I want to make it doubly safe. Them that know me know that I always play safe. I been working this game for a good many years, but outside of the little nick out of the corner of my left ear, I ain't ever been touched with a knife or a gun. That's how safe I work.

"To make this game safer still, I want to

GET YOUR 4 FREE BOOKS NOW—
A VALUE BETWEEN $16 AND $20

Mail the Free Book Certificate Today!

FREE BOOKS CERTIFICATE!

YES! I want to subscribe to the Leisure Western Book Club. Please send my 4 FREE BOOKS. Then, each month, I'll receive the four newest Leisure Western Selections to preview FREE for 10 days. If I decide to keep them, I will pay the Special Members Only discounted price of just $3.36 each, a total of $13.44. This saves me between $3 and $6 off the bookstore price. There are no shipping, handling or other charges. There is no minimum number of books I must buy and I may cancel the program at any time. In any case, the 4 FREE BOOKS are mine to keep—at a value of between $17 and $20! Offer valid only in the USA.

Name_____

Address_____

City_____ State_____

Zip_____ Phone_____

Biggest Savings Offer!

For those of you who would like to pay us in advance by check or credit card—we've got an even bigger savings in mind. Interested? Check here. ☐

If under 18, parent or guardian must sign.
Terms, prices and conditions subject to change. Subscription subject to acceptance. Leisure Books reserves the right to reject any order or cancel any subscription.

take three men with me. And there ain't any men in this section of the country but the Mornes and the Pattisons. So here I've come. Can I get three of you to go with me?"

There was a fierce humming of assent, a restless stirring of bodies and gripping of guns.

"We'll hear all about your plan, first," said Big Jim.

The outlaw gave him an ugly glance. "I want to get the bank in town," he said quietly. "The vault ain't none too new. There's a crack around its door soup would run in. And here's the soup to run."

He produced, almost carelessly, from his pocket a flask; and even Big Jim drew a faint breath when he realized that it was deadly nitroglycerine.

"And here's soap for the mold. That's all I need."

Colby had pocketed the "soup" and brought out some common, yellow laundry soap. He put it away again and smiled upon his audience.

"That's all there is to it. I get three of you to stand guard on the outside. I don't ask none of you to come inside with me. I'll do all the hard work. I'll blow the safe. I'll take all the big chances.

"I've framed the job, and I've done the

dirty work and fixed the watchman so's he won't give us no trouble. What I say is that there really ain't much need of your help. But I ain't a chance taker. I want everything fixed gilt-edged before I start a job. And when I take help along, I pay fat and I pay quick for what I get. I give you boys one half of everything I make and I keep one half for myself."

There was a murmur among the young Mornes and the Pattisons at such generosity. They blushed at the thought of accepting such unearned gold.

"What we ought to make I dunno to the penny, but I do know pretty close to the exact thing. We'll rake in about sixty thousand dollars from that bank. I got the word today about the amount there was in the safe. That's why I come hopping—to make the nab tonight.

"I'll make thirty thousand dollars. You three boys will make ten thousand dollars apiece. I guess that'll be enough to keep you living easy for a year or two, eh?" And he smiled benevolently at them all.

The lights of swift reckoning appeared flickering in the eyes of the youngsters. Ten thousand dollars! With such a sum, one could buy revolvers with pearl handles chased with gold, and golden figures for the bands of sombreros, and buy a horse so fast and strong that nothing could overtake it, and place upon that horse a saddle covered with silver. One could live like a king and spend with an open palm if one had such a sum. Their eyes swam with the very thought of it. Their brains were swayed and staggered by the effort to conceive it.

"I'll ride with you, if you'll take me," shouted every voice among the seven.

And old John Morne leaned forward in his chair, nodding his satisfaction. "It looks like a pretty good, safe job to me," he said. "Besides, it would do me a pile of good to see old Hughson stuck up high and dry."

Harrison Colby rose and threw his cigar into the fire. "We'll start right now, then," he said.

Big Jim cleared his throat, so heavily that every one turned to him. "You ain't going a foot," he said calmly. "Not a one of you boys is going a foot with Colby."

Eight pairs of eyes looked murder at the big man.

"Has he got the right to order us?" shouted Jud Pattison finally. "Ain't we sick of doing his darned farm work? Ain't we ever to—to have no fun? Are we slaves, maybe?"

"Hush up," said Colby. "Lemme talk a bit. Look here, Jim, I know that you ain't a fool. I know that you got some big scheme up your sleeve. You're going to have the boys work along here steady and patient and industrious as hell, so's other folks will begin to forget that some of the Mornes and the Pattisons was just a little mite too active riding around by night. Ain't that it? And then, when you got them sure that the Mornes are fine, law-abiding folk, you're going to begin to slide 'em out by twos and by threes and make a clean-up. But the next morning they'll be working plumb quiet and industrious on the farm ag'in.

"I know your plan, Jim. It ain't a bad one. It's a mighty good one. But why shouldn't the boys have a little fun throwed in here and there while they're working? All work and no play ain't such a good idea, Jim!"

Colby's voice was oily smooth as he announced this glib theory. It was a new light to the others; most of all it was new to Big Jim. But he saw that the wisdom which had been attributed to him, the Machiavellian patience and deceit, had greatly strengthened his position among his clansmen. Old John Morne was biting the stem of his pipe and nodding in agreement.

"Is this a safe job?" asked Jim.

"Ain't I told you about it? Am I a liar, Jim?"

"You ain't a liar, maybe. But you know and I know that any job can be framed up smooth.

160

The reason that so many gents get shot up and that so many prisons are full of 'em, is that while all their plans turn out good, the plans of other folks change.

"The watchman you think you got fixed may be double crossing you. You *know* that he may be. He's worked for Hughson for fifteen years. Hughson has took good care of his whole family when he was sick. What makes you so sure that he ain't been making a fool of you?"

"We all got to take some chances," said Colby gloomily. "Besides, he took my money. And he's sure a fool if he thinks that he ain't going to pay it back either with more coin or with the promise that he made. Them that don't pay me—well, they don't live long afterward. And the old boy knows it well enough. You can lay on that, Big Jim!"

He had restored his credit among the listeners, though it had been shaken for an instant.

Big Jim started on another track. "I remember about other parties that started out as safe as this. Let's see, what was the last time you come here, Colby?"

"A whole year since I've seen the folks," said Harrison Colby. "But the last time I come—you remember, Morne?"

"I know," said the old man, his face brightening. "It was a great piece of work."

"What was?" asked Jim.

"Why, that was the time that Harry and Mat did the job on the express safe."

Big Jim had heard of that tale, though he was away from the ranch long before it.

It was a thrilling tale of how the two men had ridden blind baggage on the train out from a small mountain station, had worked their way back, had entered the end door on the old-fashioned car with a key which Colby had secured, and then had "stuck up" the guards and blown the safe. That done, they had cleaned out the money—some forty thousand dollars—and had dropped off the train as it slowed up at the next stop.

That brilliant bit of robbery had been talked of across the whole continent.

"Nothing cooler and cleverer than that was ever done," said old John Morne, with a sigh. "Forty thousand pinched off as clean as a whistle!"

"I tell you, John, it was harder work than the job we're doing to-night, and yet there was less money in it, a pile!"

The young Mornes were furious with eagerness to get at the work.

"Wait a minute," said Big Jim. "What became of that forty thousand dollars?"

There was an instant's pause, and the bright eyes of the outlaw glared at Big Jim.

"We had some bad luck," he said gloomily. "They raised the devil in the town as soon as the train got in. They telegraphed all over the mountains. Inside of a day the whole darned range was alive with gents that was looking for us. They had a fat reward on both our heads. They sure meant business.

"We had to separate. I—I buried my money. Twenty thousand dollars in gold weights quite a pile, you know. I went through their lines and got away. But poor old Pattison, he tried to carry the coin with him. You all know what happened. It was a fool thing to do. I advised him agin' it. But he had to go ahead and work things out his own way.

"They cornered him and killed him. I only wish that he'd taken my advice. But it sure wasn't no fault of mine!"

"What happened to your twenty thousand that was buried?" asked Jim.

"Didn't you read about that? Darned if I didn't have bad luck with that, too. It was found by some fool kids that was digging to make themselves a robbers' cave. Dog-gone me if they didn't run right onto that coin. I was left all froze out."

"Well," said Jim, "that was a famous robbery. A very smooth job, Colby. But what was gained out of it? Pattison was killed, and the money was taken back."

163

"That was bad luck," admitted Colby gloomily. "But that's one time out of ten."

"You've made a lot of money, ain't you?" asked Big Jim quietly.

"Money? I could stack this room with it, from wall to wall."

At his gesture the eyes of the young Mornes widened.

"How much money have you now, Colby?" asked Big Jim.

The outlaw, seeing that he was cornered, showed his teeth and remained silent.

"You ain't got a cent," said Big Jim. "You've made a stack of money. Sure you have. But what good has it done for you? And what good have you ever done for the Mornes?

"You've taken out some of our best men. And you've left 'em dead on the trail or else you've landed 'em in prison. Them are the things that we got to thank you for, and nothing else. Understand, Colby?"

"Is that the way the rest of you feel?" asked Colby, beside himself with rage, but yet not quite able to meet the steady eye and the deep, steady voice of Conover.

There was no answer from the rest. Old John Morne was scowling at the floor. The others watched Big Jim, as though they yearned, every one of them, to take their chance on this night of nights, but dreaded

164

his displeasure.

"All right," said Colby. "But I'll take a story out that'll start some folks smiling. Eight men, but only one mind among 'em."

He put on his hat and stepped to the door.

"Do you send word to your partner, Hughson?" he asked Big Jim, sneering.

The latter considered for a dubious instant. "I'd never of knowed if you hadn't come to us an' trusted me by telling your yarn. No, I can't lift a hand to let Hughson know, but I'll tell you what I hope, Colby. I hope that the watchman has double crossed you. I hope to-night starts you on your way to jail."

"Thanks," said Colby. "I hope to-night shows the Mornes that they've stopped being men and have turned into sapheads."

CHAPTER NINETEEN

"A PRESENT FROM COLBY"

It is necessary to follow Colby through this night. Once the door had closed behind him, he shook his fist at the house and fell into a speechless frenzy of rage. Then he stole back and peered through the window. He could both hear and see. At least, the great voice of

Big Jim was plainly audible as he heaved himself out of his chair.

"I can see that you're all aching to have a talk about me. Well, lads, I'm going to give you a chance to say what you want to say. I'm going to my room. You can talk your hearts out."

He waved good night to them and left the room. And, the moment he was gone, the youngsters gathered like wolves around the large chair of John Morne.

"Has he got a right to bully us?" they demanded. "Has he got any authority over us?"

"After all," exclaimed another, "he ain't even a Morne. He ain't nothing but a stranger. Darned little he cares about us. He's just cheated us out of thirty thousand dollars. All he wanted was to be asked on that trip himself."

But old John Morne said not a word. A devil of anger was working in his face, and plainly it was not anger directed against the younger man. Yet what was in his thoughts he refrained from speaking.

"You got to know that Jim *was* asked," said the patriarch at last. "He wouldn't go. He's never done a shady thing in his life."

That silenced the complaints for the instant, but as Harrison Colby rode away that night, he knew that the reign of Big Jim among the Mornes had been seriously threatened. He would come again, before long, with some even more tempting plot. It would be more than strange if he were not able to entice the youngsters away with him.

In the meantime, he wondered about the curious dragging of the right leg of the giant as he had walked across the room. It was very odd—as a man walks when one of his legs has gone to sleep.

Yet he could not deny that Big Jim had shown good headwork in his analysis of the outlaw's life. In fact, one reason that Colby hated Conover so utterly from this time was that the latter had shown to him the exact truth about his past life and the life which must be coming. There was no future.

He knew that the years to come would be repetitions of the years through which he had already lived. There would be a long train of fights, ventures, escapes, starving poverty, and full wallets. With this bitter certainty, that when his wallet was full he would be busily flying for his life, and that the moment he reached a town the money would be taken from him by the first gambler he met.

That was the one weak link in his steel armor. He could not keep from cards, and sometimes he thought of himself, furiously, as a stupid fishing bird which toils and toils, while the gamblers waited idly and then dropped on him, like the fleet frigate bird, and made him give up his spoils.

However, he could not give up his career. He must keep on with it. He could not live six months without the excitement. And the end would come to him just as it came to all of the others of his ilk. A bullet would touch his life, or the walls of a prison would close around him.

In the meantime, as he approached the town, he determined that he would at least make use of the suggestion of Big Jim concerning the banker's watchman. The first thing he was to do was to meet the watchman, old Jeff Mullin, in the latter's house.

But he did not go straight to the front door of the place. He circled carefully to the rear, worked open the kitchen door, and slid as silently as a snake to the dining-room door, which was framed by a broken line of light, shining from the farther side.

And he heard two voices in a hasty conference.

"I'll go back now upstairs," said what Colby recognized perfectly as the voice of the sheriff. "He'll be showing up before long."

"There ain't any trouble," said the watchman. "He'll have three men with him, he said. They'll make enough noise to give you a warning. Besides, how can you protect me when you're upstairs?"

"I can't protect you anyways," said the sheriff, "if they suspect you. They'll shoot you down, Jeff. All I can do is to serve 'em up the same medicine afterward. I can revenge you, but you're taking your life in your hands if you try to double cross a gent like Colby. Mind you, it's to my interests to have you go ahead. But I got to tell you the truth."

There was a pause, and when Mullin spoke again his voice was shaken.

"I know," he said. "But I'm willing to go ahead with the thing. I was tempted. God knows that I came near falling. That money he promised me looked mighty big. And it's only right that I should go through a little danger on account of it. Have you got the boys ready at the bank?"

"I've got close on to fifty men lying around in the houses near the bank, and a dozen more in the cellar of the bank. When I give the word, they'll turn that place into a hell of flying lead. They'll turn Colby into a sieve."

"God forgive me!" whispered Mullin.

"For what?"

"For betraying a fellow man to his death."

"You talk foolish, Jeff. You're acting like any good citizen ought to act. Keep right on through with it."

The outlaw waited to hear no more. He stole out by the way in which he had come into the house.

In the dark he crouched against the wall of the house and gave himself over to a passion of hatred and rage. He turned the exquisite poignancy of his revenge over his tongue, so to speak. What he wished was chiefly that the watchman had a dozen lives so that he could have the joy of crushing out each life, little by little, with torment.

But there was no time. There was not more than enough to kill him once and get away. But he must decide on what was the manner of killing that would give most anguish of soul to Mullin, and therefore the greatest joy to himself.

As for the right to kill, he did not entertain the slightest doubts. In his own code, the crime of Mullin was the blackest that could be conceived, for a criminal who betrays his fellow criminal is destroying the very foundation and bed rock of the entire world of crime. It cannot exist without some such honest cohesion of part to part.

And Colby himself, though he had committed nearly every crime that will hang or imprison a man, had never yet been untrue to a fellow. Never had he abandoned a companion in the hour of stress. Never had he flinched

170

from a work of rescue when one of his gang had fallen.

Perhaps the reason was that unless he showed himself fearless in the behalf of his associates, his associates would not show themselves fearless on his own behalf. But, nevertheless, treason to one's comrade seemed to him like the sin of Judas over again. It made his heart ache with rage.

He finally decided on a way to kill his man. It was simple, and yet it was also perfect. In the telling, it would not be much. But in the performance it would be great indeed.

He went to the window of the room in which Mullin was sitting. The sheriff had left him. The old man sat with his face in his hands. How great the convulsion of his soul must have been, when it made his very body shake. The fingers quivered. The white hair shook. But Colby had no pity for white hair. His own would soon be silver.

Slowly, with infinite care, he raised the window. It did not make a sound. But though the noise did not alarm the watchman, those keen eyes looking in upon him from the night would do so.

With indescribable relish Colby saw the hands fall from the face of Mullin, saw him raise his head, saw him begin to turn his head by slow degrees. There was a nightmare of terror in the soul of old Mullin. It brought shining drops of perspiration to his forehead. But at length his head was moved far enough for him to make out that the window was indeed open.

He leaped to his feet with a shriek. And there, in the window, he was confronting Harrison Colby, and the outlaw was smiling in the intensity of his enjoyment.

Fear would have struck the old man to the floor. But Colby did not wait for that.

"A present from Colby, sheriff," he shouted through the house, and then, raising his gun, he shot Mullin fairly through the heart.

CHAPTER TWENTY

DOCTOR AYLARD'S OFFER

To pursue Colby was like pursuing a ferret. He seemed to dive underground and disappear. So Sheriff Al Dunning decided, finally, to use a different means of attack. He spent two days combing the country, but vainly. Harrison Colby had dropped out of sight.

The sheriff rode down with a small army and searched the premises of the Mornes. It was a ticklish encounter. The young Pattisons and Mornes flew to arms and stood about with their deadly rifles in their hands and mischief in their eyes. But no occasion came for the use of the guns.

The posse was extremely careful. It yearned for nothing better than a trace of Colby to be found and the extermination of the Mornes to follow, but no one wished to make a quarrel out of nothing. It was sure to lead to business which would be far too serious.

Moreover, they were immediately under the terrible eye of Big Jim. The bandage had been removed from his head at last. It showed a red furrow, leading from the forehead and disappearing into his hair. That hair was patched with gray about the temples. And there was a worn look of consideration about the eyes, so that Big Jim, to the crowd of man hunters, seemed more formidable than ever.

The absolute quiet in which he had lived since the doctor shot him down had not been generally taken as a sign of cowardice. For it was impossible to confront him for an instant and retain such an opinion of him.

It was held, far, and wide, that he was revolving in his mind a deep and awful scheme of revenge. As one man put it: "There'll be more than one family that'll put on mourning when Big Jim starts riding again."

For it was pointed out that he had been robbed of his horse on the same day that he was wounded. The great chestnut was still safely roaming through the country, though the men of the doctor were now busily, pursuing it.

They had run down the mares which the big fellow accumulated around him, but though their ropes fell easily upon the smaller horses, they could never get within even easy gunshot of the stallion. Rusty flew away like a wind-blown leaf at the first sign of an approach.

People freely said that the reason Big Jim did not set forth to destroy the doctor and many more, was that he was waiting until he should be able to capture his horse, for he wanted that horse beneath him when he rode forth for revenge. And, indeed, they knew that he had left the hollow already three or four times to make long excursions into the vicinity of the stallion. He had never come near the big horse, however, or otherwise it was felt that he would have been able to capture Rusty easily.

In the meantime, the pursuit of the stallion was throwing the doctor and Big Jim into opposition once more. It was even rumored that the doctor could not marry the heiress to the Stoddard Ranch until he had captured Rusty.

And yet if he captured the stallion, would he dare to hold him, knowing that the horse was the property of Big Jim?

It was of such things as these that the man hunters thought when they gazed upon Big Jim, as the latter led them through the premises of the Morne place.

They looked about them, also, with surprise and the keenest interest in the improvements which had been made. For the hollow appeared to have shrunk in size. Covered with twisting paths, dense shrubbery, great trees, and with the gloom of the name of Morne, the swamp had once seemed huge indeed. Now its face was cleared, and they saw a long and comparatively narrow depression, not much more than the three hundred acres which Big Jim claimed as its dimensions.

The big trees were down. The brush was cleared away. There was a tractor plowing out great trenches across the face of the marsh, and where the bed of the little stream drew into a steep-sided ravine farther up, a dam was being constructed.

"Almost looks to me," ventured some one, "that you're starting out to make an irrigating dam, Jim!"

To this Jim returned with a shrug of the shoulders, and the others chuckled. There was something absurd in the thought of Big

Jim doing a useful work. There was something almost degrading about it, as though a sword were to be used as an ax.

But the Mornes had changed also. Under the brief régime of Big Jim their eyes were sunken with labor and their cheeks were drawn. The flabby fat of idleness had been burned away by hard work all day and every day. Shoulders that had been inclined to slouch were beginning to square back. Appetites which could not be satisfied with moonshine whisky and bread had been developed. Beef was needed. And the hearty color in their faces showed that they fed as well as they worked.

Of course no one attributed this to mere work. It was whispered among the man hunters that Big Jim had probably organized the men for a great stroke of mischief. When that stroke fell, it would shake the very base of society on the range. It would be something like the burning of a town.

It was known, above all, that while he kept the younger generation at the hollow working, he also held them to their practice with guns every day, and had even gone so far that he established a daily prize to be contended for. Certainly there must be a sinister motive behind all of this. And by the time they finished searching the hollow, their respect for

Big Jim had swelled great.

As they departed, having found nothing, Jim drew the sheriff to one side.

"Al," he said, "I don't take this very kind, bringing out that mob!"

Dunning smiled in his face. "Why should I treat you kindly, Jim?"

"Because I'm keeping the peace."

The sheriff smiled again. "How long will it last?"

"Not long, if you treat me like a hound."

"I have a right to search where I please."

"But you know that if Colby had been here, every youngster would have died ten times over rather than see you take him away. And you know that every minute you were here, there were near a dozen guns ready to up and at you-all."

"Jim," said the sheriff suddenly, "what's the meaning of your whole game? What are you aiming at?"

"Time'll show you that."

"I'll wake up in the middle of a fire some morning, maybe. Well, I don't pretend that I can make you out. But you can lay to this, Jim. Everybody on the range has his eye on you. If you make one funny-looking move, there won't be no questions asked. We'll just come down and wipe you out."

With this not overly cheerful remark, the

sheriff rode away, and Big Jim was left to his own devices for the time being. The man hunt had come to no successful end, so the sheriff dismissed his posse.

As he dismissed it, he made a little speech in which he said that he was not going on the trail of Colby in the old way, for a few scattering days and then no more. He was going to collect a small and select band for a month's work. With that band he would go steadily on the trail. For four weeks he would plod steadily on the long trail with his men. And in four weeks' time the chances were very great that they would be able to bag their game.

It was a plan which seemed excellent to the others. Before that posse broke up, half a dozen had pledged their hands and their horses to the new scheme. Only married men, or those with businesses which would not permit a long absence, withdrew. But the best and the hardiest of the crowd stayed to see the finish.

They drew about the sheriff, when the rest had fallen away, and counted heads. Including the sheriff, they made up a band of seven.

"If we had one big gun, like Doctor Aylard," said some one, "we'd be able to go on the trail just the way we are. But in a pinch it would be pretty handy to have one fine gun

178

fighter in the crowd."

As a matter of fact, every man among them was a fine hand with weapons, but they all recognized the difference which existed between their skill and the skill of such a poisonous fighter as Harrison Colby.

So all seven turned about and rode out on the way to the Stoddard Ranch. There they streamed into the patio, found the doctor reading aloud to Jacqueline, and, in the presence of the girl, made their request.

They wanted to ride at once on the trail of Harrison Colby. Their blood was boiling since the murder of poor Jeff Mullin. But they needed the doctor with them. They would feel twice as strong and twice as sure of their work if they had him with them.

The doctor hesitated. And the more he hesitated the more their wonder grew. From the side he felt the steady and thoughtful eyes of Jacqueline upon him.

He knew that she, also, was wondering what he could do. It proved that when she saw him in the hollow, she had also marked his target practice and had seen how poor its quality was. She was wondering how he could go to face such a man as Harrison Colby. And yet, how could he refuse?

Refuse he must. If he traveled with this crowd, he was sure to have to use a weapon in their presence before he was through with them, and if he did so, with the first draw of his gun he was exposed to them as a faker.

"Friends," he said, "I'd like nothing better than to go on with you for this little party. But I can't do it. I'm very sorry, but for personal reasons I cannot go."

He regretted the speech as soon as he had made it. He was confronted with blank eyes for an instant. Then the seven interchanged glances. They could not understand, but any interpretation they could put upon the speech must have been unfavorable. He looked desperately past them. The blank horizon lay before him. Somewhere in the distance a cow, newly bereft of a calf, was bawling loudly. It seemed to the doctor a country filled with tragedy, in that moment of waiting.

"Besides," he said, fumbling to find a way out of the predicament, "it seems to me that you'll never catch a fox like this Harrison Colby when you hunt him in such a gang as this."

"How do you suggest?" asked the sheriff, with just a shade of resentment in his voice.

"Why, one or two good men, I should think, would be ample for the work. Am I wrong?"

The sheriff shrugged his shoulders. "Colby is like a cornered rat when he fights."

"Well," said the Easterner, "is Colby a fellow who'll run away from only one man?"

"From only one?" The sheriff laughed at the idea. "There ain't any one man in the country that would tackle that vermin!"

The imp of the perverse had the poor doctor by the throat. He felt that he had made a great mistake, that he had lost infinite prestige through his refusal to accompany the posse. He must make a grand gesture to redeem himself.

And there was little time.

"Why, then," he said, "I'll take a chance with Colby myself. Suppose you boys go back to town and just let people know that I'm going to take Colby myself. When the rumor gets to Colby, he'll be too much of a man to run away. He'll stay some place and wait for me. He'll have to for the sake of his name and fame. And so it will be easy enough for me to find him. When I meet him, I'll take my chance."

He forced a laugh and with a great effort made that laugh ring true.

"Sheriff, I'll try to bring your man down to you alive."

There was a little silence. Seven serious, doubting faces confronted him. It was plain that he was doubted.

"Well," said the sheriff finally, "I suppose

that there ain't any use in me saying no. It sounds like a foolish thing to try, but you know yourself and what you can do better than I do. All I can wish you is the best of good luck."

With this he departed, and the six went with him, slowly, as though they were leaving the presence of a miracle. The doctor watched them through the gate of the patio and listened until the last rattle of the hoofs had died away. Then he turned to Jacqueline.

CHAPTER TWENTY-ONE

THE IRONY OF IT

She had risen while the sheriff talked with Aylard. She was standing now beside one of the thick adobe pillars of the patio, and watching him gravely. Had there been a different concern in her eyes his heart would have leaped, but there was only an impersonal curiosity, as though she wondered at him without really caring in her heart of hearts what became of him.

"Why did you do it?" she said at length.

"I had to offer something."

"Do you know about Harrison Colby?"

182

"Not a bit."

She hesitated. "He is not like Big Jim Conover," she said.

"In what way?"

"What happened when you met Big Jim, I don't know. But the same thing won't happen with Colby. He can't miss. That's what every one knows about him."

He shrugged his shoulders. "Then," he said, braving it out, "I suppose that I mustn't miss, either."

But, in fact, he was feeling the bullet of the outlaw tear through his vitals.

She shook her head. "I've heard too many stories about Colby," she said.

"Then what can I do?" he asked.

"Not meet him. Of course you mustn't do that."

"Do you think I can flinch after what I've said?"

"You must. It would be suicide."

"I wonder, Jacqueline, if you think I have been a complete fool."

She shook her head again. "I think I understand. These people all think you a superman. And it's almost worse than death to give up that reputation."

She had gone so directly to the point that the doctor shuddered. If she began by seeing through him so easily, what would their lives be after marriage?

He knew that married happiness depends very largely on an illusion. And where no illusion existed, how could there be happiness?

And yet, even as he reasoned it out in this way, it seemed to him that she was more desirable than ever. She had never seemed so lovely. She wore a green dress, this day, and as the wind stirred it around her, she was beautiful as an angel in the eyes of the doctor.

"Jacqueline," he said, "if you really cared what happened to me, I think I should hesitate to meet Colby."

"Is that fair?" she asked him. "Is it fair to say such a thing as that?"

"It is the truth."

"It is not."

His eyes lighted.

"What do you mean?"

"I mean that I care very greatly."

"This is a wild wine to me, Jack. Why do you care?"

"Because, take it all in all, I think you are the bravest man I've ever seen."

"That's a great thing to say."

"But I have to temper it."

"Very well, tell me the whole truth."

"Then I have to confess that perhaps you're a very vain man, too, Doctor Aylard."

"Vanity drives me on?"

"Doesn't it?"

"I suppose it does. But vanity drives all of us, don't you think?"

"Will you tell me," she said suddenly, "what happened when you met Big Jim?"

"There were twenty people who saw what happened," he said, cleverly avoiding the question.

"I know—I know! But still there's a mystery."

"Why?"

"You see, I know Big Jim. I know all about him. I saw him and talked to him about five years ago. And he's the sort of a man who can't go down. He can't fail. It isn't in him to fail."

She spoke with a heightened color.

"One would almost think that you're fond of him?" he suggested cautiously.

"I am," she admitted. "Tremendously. Because with all his strength he has such a gentle heart—like a child's heart, Clinton. You'd never guess, knowing him only as you do."

"Perhaps he has imposed on you."

He was drawing her out, for this flush of enthusiasm had so changed her that he could hardly recognize her as the same woman. If only she had been looking at him, speaking of him, he would have been in a seventh heaven of happiness. But she was staring past him, as

185

though the formidable shape of Big Jim were actually in her eyes.

"He couldn't do that," she said quietly.

"You're sure?"

"There are times," she said, very thoughtfully, "when one sees into people and sees all that is in them—just a glance. I think I've seen Big Jim."

"And found nothing really wrong in him?"

"Nothing," she said.

He was startled. All that she had said had not prepared him for such a wild statement as this.

"Do you know what they are saying of him now?" he suggested.

"What are they saying?"

"That he's making ready to get his revenge on me."

Her answer was another shock.

"Do you blame him for that?"

"Well, that's a hard question to answer."

"I mean that if you'd been beaten by another man, would you rest until you had made yourself square with him?"

"If you put it in that way, of course not. But isn't this a little different? He's training all of the men in Morne hollow, they say. When he starts, he'll ride with a whole band of young murderers behind him."

"I don't think so."

"Then what does it mean—this long quiet in the hollow?"

"Are you going to condemn a man for keeping the peace?"

"That's not fair. Of course I don't. I'm simply telling you the conjectures of people who know the Mornes and Big Jim much better than I possibly can."

She was silent.

"You're not convinced?" he asked.

She shrugged her shoulders.

"But about Colby?" she said, and as she drew him back to the original point of the conversation he knew at once that she did not wish to tell him all that was in her mind.

It was a revelation to him. It showed him, in a lightning flash of understanding, that she cared for him so little that even a ruffian, a Big Jim Conover, was more to her than he was.

It did not change his regard for her. It merely gave more shadowing to his conception of her character. It showed him that she was more truly a daughter of the range than he had dreamed.

But it did not alter the glamour of her being for him. It deepened his knowledge of Big Jim, however, immensely. There was more to that man than he had guessed. For he had felt that the big man was simply a stepping-stone on which he climbed to greatness or something like it, but now he began to comprehend that there was much more to him. If the big fellow had the power to create such an enthusiasm in the breast of a girl like Jacqueline, then it was plain that he was more than a mere gun fighter. What were his other qualities?

He determined on the spot that when occasion served he would study the other with the greatest care. Perhaps there might even be some things which he could learn from him—characteristics which had interested Jacqueline, and by which the doctor himself could profit.

"About Colby," he said in answer to her question. "I'm going to do nothing for a time. I'm going to wait until the news of what I intend can get to me. Then, unless I'm very greatly mistaken, word will come that he's waiting for me, some place or other."

That was the end of the conversation on this day. He had hoped that she would talk more —that she would attempt to dissuade him. But she did not. She simply hesitated for a time, and then she went away with her head bowed a little, as though in rather painful thought.

What that thought could be, he would have given a great deal to know, but he had no chance to see much of her during the next day or two. He was too thoroughly occupied with the rancher.

For when Stoddard heard what his future son-in-law intended concerning Harrison Colby, he fell into a frenzy of concern. He began by keeping the doctor up till past midnight on that very day. And in the library of the big ranch house he thrashed the question back and forth. It was folly of the worst sort, he assured Aylard, for him to go on the trail of the murderous Colby alone. For it was like entering the lists barehanded against a rattlesnake. He would fight honestly, but Colby was sure to use unfair methods.

"You're wrong," the doctor would say. "It's the first time in his life that Colby has ever received a fair challenge or anything like it. He's been hunted like a rat. Now that he gets a summons to fight, man to man, you'll see that he answers it. He'll be complimented by the news."

And the doctor was right, even to his own astonishment. He had really expected, in spite of what he said, that the outlaw would not be heard of again in that district.

But the third day brought strange news. Colby had appeared in Saylor's saloon and gaming house in the new mining camp among the mountains at Twin Falls. He had come by night, and, from the doorway of the saloon, he had announced that he would come to a table in the place every night after that and wait for the arrival of the braggart doctor who was coming on his trail single-handed.

How that was possible, the doctor hardly understood. He could not see that every man in that mining camp, including the deputies of the law, would understand that here was a fight between man and man—that they would respect the courage of Colby in coming down to accept the challenge, and that not a hand would be raised against the outlaw.

But what was apparent to the doctor was that he must immediately start for Twin Falls to accept the proffered battle, or else all of his glory would be gone.

And the irony of it lay in the fact that when he went, he must fight his battle with wooden guns.

CHAPTER TWENTY-TWO

TWIN FALLS

It was the meeting between the doctor and Colby that made Twin Falls famous. The gold mines had proved to be far too limited in extent to admit of many strikes. It could never be a popular field. And though many thousands of dollars' worth of powder were burned and many tons of ground broken, there was little return. There was much "color," but it seldom led into pay dirt.

However, the gold rumor had been strong enough, as usual, to attract a rush. Several thousands plunged into the narrow gulch which had a waterfall tumbling and sparkling and roaring at either end.

Those currents met in the center of the gulch with a great crashing which made a distinct murmur to the farthest ends of the valley. And, indeed, there was never a time when the murmur of the water courses or of the falls did not beat in upon the minds of men, and, being inescapable, those sounds became oppressive.

It was not a place for guilty men, that valley. For the very air trembled with a feeling of danger, of retribution ahead.

Even law-abiding citizens became thoughtful after a day in the sprawling town which stretched for a mile along the river. Their consciences were awakened, and they remembered small sins of omission and commission. For the muttering of the water—continually changing in volume as the wind blew the sounds to and fro and made them far or distant—was a threat suspended over every head.

In the meantime, there was the usual assembling of young and old fortune hunters who came prepared to dig in the ground, but most of all was the number of rascals who came never dreaming of digging a shovelful of rock, but who were there to prey like jackals on the honest work of the lions who toiled in the stone and ripped the gold out of the stiff fingers of the earth.

There were dance halls enough, with saloons and gaming rooms attached, for the amusement of the hard workers. But in all the town there was one saloon which surpassed the others in that it had attained a good name. This was Saylor's.

Having acquired a name for honesty, it straightway lost all patronage. For the cheats would not, of course, patronize a place in which crooked card games were not looked upon with favor, and the honest people, of course, would not go to a place where the easy, manners and the pleasant ways of crooked gamblers were missing.

For honest men, particularly honest laborers, hunt for the bait which has the hook concealed in it. They are not only gullible, but they are blind, and they insist upon being deceived. For the very reason that Saylor's was known to be honest it was suspected of being dull, and that suspicion killed his business.

The savings of half a lifetime, which had been honestly made in a rather dishonest business, were swept away. Saylor was hanging on, so to speak, by the tips of his fingers. And then came Harrison Colby with his startling announcement.

He had chosen Saylor's because it was the quietest place in the town. He had chosen the town because in that wild bit of the frontier he was least apt to be molested. But the moment he delivered his challenge, Saylor's became the most important place of amusement in the town.

Every evening, from eight o'clock until ten, Harrison Colby came out of the mountains and sat behind a corner table in Saylor's house smoking his long, thin, black cigars, watching the front door of the house through which his enemy must come, listening to the hum of voices, feeling the curious, horrified, fascinated eyes of the crowd, and always aware, in the back of his mind, of the dolorous rolling of the water, far away.

Saylor's was packed with the curious. The news of the strange and silent drama spread far and wide. People washed down like spring floods out of the mountains and came to stare at a man who was patiently waiting to kill or to be killed.

It made little difference that he was one

with a reputation worse than that of a wild beast. What was important, for the nonce, was his iron nerve. He was taking a chance that the officers of the law would be sporting enough to hold off their hands and let this strange duel go through. And his opinion of them was justified. They did not stir to annoy him. They even doffed their stars and came to gaze in their turn at the hero.

For such the gun fighter and outlaw became. Young men and old watched him and worshiped the cool scorn for danger which enabled him to wait here so calmly.

But there was another actor in the drama who was even more important than the outlaw, and this was the tenderfoot who had delivered the challenge, and who was coming to strike at the great Harrison Colby.

The story was told with many variations how Doctor Aylard had calmly told the sheriff, who came asking him to be a member of a posse, that he could not go at that time, but that he would take into his own hands the little matter of attending to the capture of Harrison Colby.

It showed either an immense and fatuous conceit, or else it was a touch of heroic self-confidence. And to back the belief that it was the second state and not the first, it was pointed out that he had already met and conquered a fighter no less celebrated than Big Jim Conover. Indeed, five years ago it was stated that he had been even more famous and dreaded than Harrison Colby himself.

In fact, people began to feel that the doctor was a sort of Achilles, made for great deeds and an early death. Moreover, he was a unique. Other men had done great things and performed rare adventures in the West, but none had been so strangely out of the picture—so completely the learned man, the cultured gentleman, the outlander.

It irritated the rough cow-punchers a little to think that a man of such species should outdo even their greatest heroes. But, nevertheless, they yearned to cast their eyes upon the great man.

In the meantime, the great man was making slow preparations for the journey. What he wanted above all to do was to capture the chestnut stallion, Rusty, and then marry Jacqueline.

After this he would make the journey, having achieved his greatest ambition before starting. For he had a fatal feeling that he was riding to his death. How could he feel otherwise, knowing that he was armed with only the wooden guns of bluff and that he was going forward to face weapons of steel?

He persuaded Stoddard to lend him every

cow-puncher on the ranch. He hired a score of other men in the town. He rented a hundred good horses and saddles and distributed them through the mountains. He gave five dollars a day to every man in the service. He promised a thousand dollars to the man who should first lay a rope upon the stallion.

Above and beyond all this, he even let the great secret escape in order to increase the zeal of the horse hunters, and he let it be known that, owing to a careless bet, he could not marry Jacqueline Stoddard until he had captured the horse.

It caused an immense excitement. In the first place, there had never been such a focusing of exciting events since men could remember.

In the mountains waited an enemy ready to destroy the doctor, but here in the hills the doctor furiously pursued his ambition of becoming married. Was he to marry and then ride off to such a great danger?

When they asked him about it, he merely laughed. In fact, he was forced to pretend to despise the danger, otherwise he would have been considered the worst sort of a cad!

"Colby is a rat," he told every one. "He's murdered men. He's never fought with them. When I meet him he'll curl up like a dog and beg for mercy. You'll see that it will turn out that way. He doesn't dare to face me."

They brought news of this statement to Harrison Colby. He turned as white as birch bark. His eyes glared at the informant.

"Did he say that?" said Harrison Colby, with that soft voice which goes with a spasm of the utmost fury in some men. "Did he say that?"

He had no other comment to make. And no other comment was necessary. Men felt assured that they would see a battle of giants when the meeting took place.

But now came the hunt of Rusty. It was to be a tremendous affair. Besides the hired men, a full three-score of good-natured men volunteered to do their best for the happiness of Jacqueline and the doctor.

First the sheriff rode over to Morne hollow and interviewed Big Jim.

"What'll happen if they catch Rusty?" he said. "Will you claim the hoss after it's run wild and free this way and you ain't been able to catch him? Will you claim the hoss, providing that they offer you a good price and a fair price for him?"

"I don't give a darn for the price," said Big Jim. "If they catch Rusty, they're welcome to him."

"But they're sure to do it," explained the sheriff. "Half the county has turned out to hunt him. They got him surrounded now in the hills with a big circle. All they got to do is to collapse the sides of that there circle, and they got the hoss. It just takes care. It don't take no more."

Big Jim laughed. "Go ahead and help 'em hunt," he said. "I'll give you a hundred dollars, and I'll give 'em the hoss for a wedding present if they can catch him."

"You don't think they will?"

"Never!"

"Give us your guess on what'll happen when Colby meets up with the doctor?"

"The doctor has to win."

"How come?"

"Because it ain't meant that Colby should beat him. He's being saved for somebody else."

There was no need for him to elaborate to make his meaning the more clear. It was plain that he himself intended to have an affair with the doctor before many days. So the sheriff went off to carry the exciting news to the horse hunters before they began to hunt.

But Big Jim remained in Morne hollow and went off among the hills. There, for a whole hour, he practiced with his left hand. His draw was fast; his shot was sure. But oh, how slow, how dull, how blunderingly wild were those shots compared with the magic which had once lain in his right hand!

He tried that right hand, at last. Had not the doctor told him that he must try it every day, once?

He made the draw. Behold, the gun leaped forth with the lightning ease of old.

But when his finger was closing on the trigger, all the strength went out of the arm. The gun twisted awry. The bullet plunged into the ground not a quarter of an inch from the toe of his boot!

And Big Jim cast up his hands before his face with a groan and fled through the hills blindly, dragging that numb, right leg.

CHAPTER TWENTY-THREE

NO NEED FOR GUNS

The next morning they began the hunt for Rusty. They started shrinking the circumference of the circle. It was said that before the hunt began, two hundred men were mounted. And there were groups of fresh horses posted here and there through the hills, in case there should be a chance to run the great stallion if he should break away.

They caught sight of him. He headed back

into the trap. He shot out on the other side, sighted the horsemen, and flung back again.

Again he caromed to the farther side of the circle, with his splendid head flung high and the sun glittering along his sweat-shining body. Again he was headed, but now he only hesitated and flinched back for an instant. All around him he could perceive the circle closing. He could hear their shouts of triumph.

He picked out the nearest approach to a gap in the line. The cow-punchers were galloping in like madmen, now, and the line was no longer even. Each man had in his mind's eye the thousand dollars which fell to him who first put a rope on the stallion. They came swinging their ropes, yelling, with battle in their eyes. And where the widest gap appeared was, unfortunately, at the very weakest point in the circle.

That was where Stoddard and Aylard himself rode. Aylard, of course, hardly knew one end of a rope from the other. And Stoddard had not used a lariat for years. They had ropes, of course, but these were rather for show than for actual work.

And at this gap Rusty determined to plunge. But first, like an Indian, he determined to make a feint, and he delivered a typical Indian charge.

Like an animal maddened with fear, he made straight at a close knot of punchers. What a picture he made as he raced along, with the wind tossing his mane straight up, and every muscle in his glorious body working. The sun flashed on his silken flanks, and the devil was in his eyes.

Cow-punchers split apart, their ropes ready, their canny cow ponies high-headed and sharp-eyed for the game ahead. They made an open funnel, but if the chestnut darted down it a dozen ropes would shoot at him.

That was not the mark in the mind of Rusty, however. Suddenly he dodged to one side, as a football player dodges when he runs through an open field. And then, like a bullet, he was off for the gap between the doctor and the rancher. There was a shout of alarm.

The rancher, with an oath, shook out his noose and made ready for the cast, but instead of running past him, the stallion aimed straight at Stoddard, his mouth open, his teeth gleaming, his ears flat along his neck.

Who can rope a charging horse? Stoddard veered to one side to make his cast. And at that instant the chestnut swerved again and was through the gap like lightning. The rope of Stoddard flapped idly against his flank. It added wings to the stallion's speed, as he fled.

It was not the end. For two hours they rode furiously in pursuit. The outer watchers took up the chase. Horses were changed. But still it was of no avail. At the end of the two hours he was out of the circle, he was out of the mountains, and racing freely through the rolling hills, and the prophecy of Big Jim had proven correct.

There were many curses, many dark faces on that day, and perhaps the only voice that sang was that of Jacqueline when the news was brought to her. As for the doctor, there was nothing left for him but to start for Twin Falls.

He dressed for the part he was to play. He wore not a cow- puncher's costume, but a pair of cord riding breeches, a neat flannel shirt, and a black bow tie, a pair of leather puttees, and a narrow-brimmed black felt hat. Around his waist a revolver was belted. Thus equipped, with a small pack rolled behind his English pad, he started from the ranch.

He made a foothill town that night, slept there, and started slowly on at noon of the next day. For he wanted the news of his approach to precede him. That was part of his plan. Everything that he did must be known in the mining town long before he arrived. Otherwise all of his good scheming would be for naught. And he had naught but his scheme with which to fight this approaching battle; he had naught but the wooden gun of a sham.

It was a sober time for the doctor, this interval of his approach to the town of Twin Falls. It was a time in which he frequently reviewed his life and his deeds, and once or twice a tear rose in his eye at the thought that an Aylard should die here, unlamented, in an obscure mining town of the West.

He even considered turning back, but his courage was too real to admit of that. Besides, he had begun to have a blind faith in his luck, since his advent into the West. Luck would stand by him. Luck would carry him through even this great crisis.

According to his plan, it was dark when he rode down the slope into the gulch of Twin Falls. He paused at the head of the valley to have his supper with the first group of miners he encountered. They learned his name two minutes after he arrived, and one of their number stole away and raced down the gulch to the town. There he rushed into Saylor's and told his story.

And all eyes turned upon Harrison Colby. He had but just entered and sat down at his accustomed table, facing the outer door of the house. Perhaps Saylor himself was the only man who had any sympathy for the outlaw at that moment. For money had rushed into his pockets through the coming of Colby, and, no matter how the fight terminated, thousands would flock afterward to see the historic site of the encounter. In a word, the fortune of Saylor was made.

Though, as an honest man, he could not like Colby, yet he could not but feel a pang of regret at the thought that his benefactor might fall in the ensuing fight.

As for Colby, he could not help but know that there was a meaning in the silence which had spread over the place. The games of cards ended. The men at the bar turned gloomy, staring eyes upon him. When they spoke to one another it was in faint voices.

There was nothing to compete with the heavy rolling of the waters in the distance, and these beat ominously into the room. And every rumble of those waters was like a prophecy of death. It was in vain that Colby told himself the death was to be that of Aylard. It was in vain that he told himself that he could not fail. There was an inward prompting which filled him with weakness.

It was the suspense which had accumulated into a ton's weight, dragging at his nerves. He could see, now, that he had played a madman's part in coming to this place and waiting, night after night. The first one had been easy enough. The second one had been much worse. And now he found that his reserve of confidence was exhausted.

How long would this battery of eyes play upon him, like buzzards circling in the heavens and waiting for a death?

Suddenly he rapped on his table and called for whisky. There was a drawn breath around the room, and he understood what it meant. They saw through him. He was losing courage and had called for a stimulus before the crisis.

Colby wanted to countermand his order, but he dared not do that. The whisky came. He drank it at a gulp, and though he was a man who drank very little, the stuff tasted merely like a bad-flavored water to him. It did not sting his throat or bring a mist to his eyes. Whisky had been intolerable to him before this night. But now it was a mere nothing.

He snapped the glass away from him and sat back, lighting another cigar. He began to study the faces. They were all hostile, all excited, all rather disgusted, as though he were already a dead thing.

Colby closed his right hand to press away the chill of horror which was invading him. That right hand must not be affected by anything. That right hand, which dealt at cards and which used his revolver—what would happen to him if it should fail to do its duty?

205

He stared at it so long and so hard that the fingers began to tremble. Had others seen that sign of weakness?

A door closed. He looked up suddenly, his eyes wide. No, it was not Doctor Aylard, but every eye now seemed to have a hidden knowledge about him. Somewhere in the distance a voice was speaking. Its sound was as the voice of old Jeff Mullin!

"No more of that!" said the outlaw softly to himself. And he added immediately: "I'm talking to myself, and that shows that my guts are gone. Does it show that? Do these gents know? Is that why they're staring so hard?"

Jeff Mullin was dead, he told himself. He had heard the details of the funeral, even. Besides, he knew that his bullet had found the heart of the old watchman. There was no crime in that.

Certainly he had been justified in taking the life of the man who had double crossed him. If it were only Mullin that he had to answer for—but there were others, a long procession of them.

"No more of this!" gasped out the outlaw to himself. "If he'd only come now——"

There was a faint buzzing in his ears. There was a faint mist before his eyes.

"It's the whisky," he told himself. "Oh, fool that I am! It's the whisky that's unnerving me.

It's putting me to sleep——"

The swinging door creaked again. He half rose from his chair. Then he settled heavily back in it and gripped the butt of his gun, for it was Doctor Aylard!

There was no doubt about him—a big, cool-eyed, proud-acting gent. That was the way the doctor had been described, and the description was perfect. He was very tall indeed, and very broad.

So much the better for a quick snapshot, when he had a target such as this to fire at. He certainly could not miss. And yet there was a meaning in the careless good nature of the doctor. He seemed to be swallowing a smile continually, as though he knew a hidden thing which made all the difference!

What could it be?

"There'll be drinks all around," said the doctor in a clear and even voice from the bar.

Drinks were set up, and still all in the same deadly silence.

"You're not drinking," asked Saylor respectfully, when the other glasses were brimming.

"I'm not drinking," said the doctor. "I never drink when I have a bit of work to do."

And he laughed so frankly and openly that others were able to join in that laughter as well.

Harrison Colby wondered vaguely at it. He began to moisten his lips, which were very dry.

"I'm not drinking," said the doctor.

CHAPTER TWENTY-FOUR

A SPY

The doctor intended to rush straight back to the ranch, where the full weight of his new glory might come to bear upon Jacqueline and her mind might be more opened to the full worth of her husband to be.

But he could not go back at once. In the first place, the town of Twin Falls turned out for him as if he had been a king. For, coming upon the heels of his victory over Big Jim, the conquest of Colby was not doubly but tenfold convincing.

One success may be the result of chance or foolish hazard, but two great victories have a cause behind them. People began to understand the cause, they told one another. The vast force of the will of Doctor Aylard, united with his skill with weapons, was what beat down resistance.

And astonishing as had been the defeat of

Big Jim, the crushing of Harrison Colby, without a gun drawn, had been too horrible to even talk about. No one referred to the details of it. But though the victory was so great that it was degrading to human nature to recall it, yet there was all the more applause for the doctor.

People began to have a sort of superstitious reverence for him. It was held that he possessed a power almost akin to hypnotism. That idea was freely circulated. And people were willing to give it credence.

It was so generally believed, indeed, that very brave men, very famous men, did not hesitate to say that it was not shameful to refuse battle with such a man as the doctor. It was rather the part of wisdom than of cowardice. And when Western cowmen made such remarks, it could be understood that Doctor Aylard had been placed on a pinnacle apart.

Men journey for days for the mere sake of shaking hands with him and looking into his face. The young men came with awe. The old men came and forgot their reminiscences of heroes of another day. For Doctor Aylard was unique. There had been great warriors of the past, but where could a man be pointed out who conquered by the weight of a single glance?

The story of how he walked calmly across the room and dragged Colby out of the chair was really too terrible to repeat. So that men referred grimly to the "thing that happened in Saylor's place," and let it go at that. And inference made the deed become a gigantic legend.

A rich lumberman secured the doctor for three days and entertained him sumptuously. A miner with millions took him next and fêted him. It was seen that the doctor was not only a tremendous fighter and a man of mystery, but that he also was so exceedingly modest that he never referred to his actions, never talked of guns, and never could even be induced to display his skill in firing at a target.

He preferred to ride through the mountains and talk about their beauty like a tourist.

He had only one weakness, and that was forgivable in a hero. It was discovered that he liked to talk about the ancient Aylard family, and how he traced his blood in a distinct strain as far back as the Conquest, and how the family name then disappeared in the mists of early Norman history, and of how his remote ancestors were probably those bearded ruffians who, sailing from the fiords of Norway and the cold seas of the North, had rushed around the world, pulling down kingdoms and setting them up anew.

Such talk might be smiled at, but it was entertaining, and the doctor told it in such fiery earnestness that it was plain he was not posing.

It was learned that if he had his right he would have the title of viscount. This made the roughhanded Westerners squirm. But they shrugged their shoulders and continued to listen. After all, he had enough dignity, enough grace, enough manliness to carry even a title without becoming effeminate.

He was detained for three weeks in this fashion among the mountains, before he could break away and come back to the Stoddard Ranch. And when he came it was like the homecoming of a second Odysseus.

The town turned out for him. And when he announced that it was like coming back to his own country after an absence in a strange land, there was not a man within miles who did not feel that he had been personally complimented by such a remark.

Aylard found occasion to pause for a half hour in the blacksmith shop and talk to the smith, not about his great deeds, but about the smith's own art.

When he rode out again, the smith could hardly contain himself. And when the story was known it was universally declared that Doctor Aylard was a good fellow of the first

211

water. For the doctor was beginning to learn the arts of kingship.

Then he passed on to the Stoddard Ranch. Stoddard shook hands with him with tears of admiration in his eyes; but it was not Stoddard he wanted to see, it was Jacqueline, and Jacqueline was not in sight.

"She didn't expect you back quite so quick," said Stoddard. "Thought it would take you longer to come out from town, most like."

Doctor Aylard excused himself as soon as he could and went out on a fresh horse to trail the girl. Every day of the three weeks he had yearned for her. And yet he had stayed away, dreading the meeting with her almost as much as he wished for it.

He told himself that if her eyes were so coldly curious now as they had been when he left her, it would be impossible for him to face her and urge on the marriage.

It was not very difficult to follow her. The cook had seen the direction she took across the hills. He passed on and caught the marks of her horse in the sand. After that, he had only to hold in that direction. She rode straight and fast, not as though she were simply out for the air; she rode, indeed, as though she were striving to get as far from the house and the doctor as possible.

He bit his lip as this thought came to him, but he went on to the edge of a valley among the hills. There he looked down upon a picture which was strange indeed.

For he saw the famous red chestnut, Rusty, running here and there through the gulley like a great dog at play, and riding slowly, side by side, through the center of the hollow, were no others than Big Jim and Jacqueline!

He could not believe his eyes, at first. But the thought that it was still Big Jim who was beating him in spite of their battle together which the doctor had won, was maddening Aylard.

It seemed as though the fellow were his Nemesis, and that he whose fall had made the stepping-stone to the doctor's greatness would be his undoing also.

So he studied the pair of them grimly, and to do it more safely, he dismounted, tethered his horse, and crept forward where he could lie on his belly behind a low outcropping of rocks. So he saw the two ride slowly down the valley toward him, and as they came he noted the clumsy, fumbling gestures which Big Jim made with his right hand.

How strange it was that every one in the range did not see the difference between him and the normal man; but it was the old and grim repute of Jim Conover, alias Morne,

213

which screened him from accurate observation.

He was leaning close to the girl. He was talking to her with the utmost energy. Ah, what a picture they made as they came closer, Conover so huge of shoulder, with his great, weather-stained throat, and a careless old hat flopping on his head. His face was more marked than ever. The rumble of his voice seemed deeper, graver. He talked almost as though he were angry with her, yet it was plain that he was only wrestling with an idea.

Aylard would have given a year of life if he could have overheard a single word, for what the big man was saying had made the girl lift her head, and she went past the spy, smiling, her eyes fixed mistily upon a happy distance, her hands clasped tightly together.

And when they were past, it seemed to the doctor that the postures of their heads were even more expressive than the full face view. For she was tilted in her saddle, ever so slightly, as though something drew her to Jim Conover.

"By the heavens," he said at last, as he came reeling to his feet and watched them out of sight around a curve of the hill, "she loves Conover!"

A dry voice immediately behind him said:

214

"Any fool could see that with just the half of an eye, eh?"

He wheeled sharply around and saw that dried up, withered bit of old humanity who had come into that part of the country as the friend and the companion of Big Jim.

It was Buck, and he was grinning down at the doctor in such an unfriendly way that Aylard forgot the shame of the position in which he had been discovered.

"What the devil do you mean?" he rumbled at Buck.

"By what?" said Buck.

"By—by spying on me like this!" thundered the doctor.

"Spying?" said Buck. "Me?"

Doctor Aylard ground his teeth, but being so completely in the wrong he could say no more. And the more he encountered the bright and steady eyes of the old man the more uncomfortable was the small of his back.

Apparently Buck did not carry a revolver either on his saddle or by his right thigh. He was armed only with a rifle. But this was a repeater, and it was handled with such a careless dexterity that the doctor's uneasiness increased.

He wanted with all his might to say something more; but the old man put it into words for him.

"How much am I offered?" he asked. "What do you pay me to keep under my hat what I know?"

"Eh?" said the doctor.

The other blurted out the brutal truth.

"Shall I go around telling folks how I seen the doctor lying on his belly and spying on the girl that he's trying to marry?"

"You infernal——" began the doctor. His voice fell away to a groan as he saw the full meaning. Such a story would smudge his fame instantly. A hero among men but a fool among women—that was what they would say of him.

"My friend," he said, "if a little money can help you, you can count on me."

"For how much?" asked Buck.

"Why, I can let you have a twenty spot——"

"Son," said Buck quietly, "this here news is worth a million dollars to my friend Big Jim. If you want to bid for it, you want to start in right high."

And the doctor knew that he was being mocked.

CHAPTER TWENTY-FIVE

A MAN OF HONOR

He had a feeling that he must either silence or chastise this difficult old man, but he could not tell how he should accomplish either end. All that he could think of in the end was the childish expedient of turning his back upon Buck and riding away.

In all his life, this was the lowest moment. That he had played the part of a sneak would be noised abroad before that day was over, and the first deathblow would have been aimed at his reputation.

Besides, he knew beyond a shadow of a doubt, unless the expressions of faces seen at close hand meant nothing at all, that Jacqueline was deeply in love with Big Jim. To crown all of his misery, he now had been checked and outfaced by an old range rider.

He determined that he could not go back to the ranch or to the town until there had been time for that story to get in, and understanding perfectly well that bad news travels upon wings, he was inclined to believe that the full details would be there within the hour.

In the meantime there was the puzzle of Rusty. After all, it was not a great one. He was simply like many dogs, wild and intractable with other men, but perfectly docile with his master.

He roved the hills freely, formed his bands of followers, and when these were scattered or run down, he veered back to find his master again and came, perhaps, to the head of Morne Valley.

What a doubly sharp sting there was in that knowledge. For it meant that Jack had the great chestnut almost at her finger tips when she willed it, though she still made the capture of the stallion by the doctor the preliminary to her wedding with him; and Big Jim let the horse run loose for the same reason, to dangle an unapproachable bait before Aylard.

There was murder in the heart of the doctor by the time he came to the top of the next range of hills. And there he found another picture which was not calculated to improve his temper. For he found himself looking down upon Morne Hollow, and what a change was there.

The forest was gone, now, saving where the big trees clustered for shade around the group of houses at the end of the depression. The mass of willows and shrubbery had disappeared also. In the place of the wilderness

218

there was now revealed a broad and gentle slope, nearly two miles long.

It was crossed with irrigating checks. Down a tangle of little ditches water was glistening even then, for some of the checks had been flooded the night before, it seemed.

Of that long expanse of farm land reclaimed, the majority had newly come from under the plow, but there was a group of small checks near him in which cultivating and sowing had been finished and the loamy surface of the ground was covered with a sprinkling of yellow-green points. A crop was coming up there, thick and fast, and the appearance of those spear points of green meant that the real battle of Big Jim was over. He could show results, now; and though the whole thing could be very easily explained, as a piece of perfectly simple reclamation that should have been carried out long before, still there was an element of the miraculous about it from which the doctor could not escape.

He swung down the hill ridge until he was within easier view of the houses in the hollow. They had been changed even as greatly as the face of the hollow itself. Sturdy additions had been built to the houses here and there. All were freshly painted.

The clearings among the trees showed a thick and even surface of lawn growing. The community of the Pattisons and the Mornes had changed from a wretched group of shacks to a pleasant little circle of houses.

As he looked down upon the picture, the doctor could understand how Jacqueline had come to admire and love Big Jim. For whereas he, the doctor, had stormed across the horizon as a conqueror of men, Big Jim had left his old ways and quite settled down as a redeemer of lost country and of lost men.

He swung back toward the ranch again, but did not have to go all the way to it, for on the road he met a buckboard driven by one of the punchers. He told the fellow to go on to the ranch, pick up three or four of the best men he could find, and give them orders from the doctor to ride to the head of Morne Valley.

"We've been hunting too high in the mountains," said the doctor. "Go hunt through the hills around the head of Morne Hollow. If you sight Rusty from the top of one of those gulches, you can rope him as he runs past, they're so small."

Having given this order, he turned back toward the town, journeying slowly. On the way he cantered up beside a farmer, bunched over in the seat of his buggy which sagged to one side, while the cowhide boot of the man dangled over the edge. It was the same fashion which the doctor had observed in Stoddard upon his first arrival. He drew down his horse to a jog and opened conversation.

It was not hard to do. The rancher blinked at the sight of Aylard as though he were surrounded by a dazzling light. It was plain that he recognized the doctor and was flattered by an opportunity to talk with him. So Aylard swung the conversation straight to the subject of the Mornes and the Pattisons. He had seen Morne Hollow, he said, and he had admired the change. It had struck him as remarkable.

"It would be a lot," declared the rancher, "if he done no more than put all them acres under the plow; but dog-gone me if I don't think that he's done more. Dog-gone me if I don't think he's leveled off them Mornes and Pattisons and took a lot of the foolishness out of 'em."

"Suppose they're only playing possum?" suggested the doctor.

"You mean that they might bust out ag'in? I don't think so. They know that the first move one of 'em makes with a gun, even if he's in the right, is going to be the last day of living for every last man of 'em. We've all stood enough from 'em. No, they ain't going to bust out.

"They like excitement, but they can't help seeing that they got it dead easy after what Big Jim has done for 'em. And they'd rather sit

221

back and live easy for a while than go out and raise hell and trouble. They've all got good clothes, good hosses, good roofs, good beds, good chuck. What more can anybody ask?"

"Does every one else think that Big Jim has really reformed 'em?" asked the doctor curiously.

"We're all a-sitting and a-waiting, Doctor Aylard. We dunno which way the cat will jump. But we're hoping. Big Jim is what we're trusting in. He's holding the reins, and he sure knows how to drive hosses and men."

He wagged his head from side to side with the weight of his convictions as he spoke.

"Though after all," he added, "some of us say that you're the one that gets the credit, doctor. If you hadn't beaten Jim, maybe he never would of changed himself and all the others."

To this the doctor could not reply.

"How did he do the work?" asked the doctor. "Did he have to plaster the hollow up to the neck with mortgages in order to have the clearing and the leveling done?"

"That clearing dog-gone near paid for the leveling," said the rancher. "Them trees were worth a pile of money. Oh, Jim owes Hughson quite a pile of money, I guess, but Hughson will be paid off with the first crop that comes in."

"What is the value of that land per acre; can you tell me?"

"Some says three hundred and some says five hundred an acre. If Big Jim plants oranges, it'll go up to a thousand dollars an acre, there ain't no doubt."

This was all that the doctor wanted to hear and a little more. He spurred on toward the town. As he saw the story now, he had been the impetus which had started Big Jim rolling in the direction of a peaceful life, and once started in that way, Big Jim had proved a great weight of accumulating force.

Romantic as was the story of the exploits of the doctor, how could they be of greater interest than the story of the reform of Big Jim? To Jacqueline it must be like the realization of a dream into fact.

And as the hoofs of his horse beat heavily on the way to town, the doctor fixed his will. Big Jim must go down. He must go to ruin among the ruins of the work that had been his. Not only did the doctor see the thing that must be done, but he saw, also, the way that the labor must be performed.

Full of this entrancing hope, he wandered up the steps of the veranda of the hotel.

He had almost forgotten that he had come to town to learn if any rumors had yet come in. But the eyes which encountered his as he advanced were as full of respect as ever. There was neither suspicion nor, worst of all, amusement in them. The story had not yet come in, then. But what could have held it back? Why had it been suppressed?

He paused on the verge of the veranda to think it over. As for the white-headed rider, there was no doubt that Buck would have told the tale far and wide, at once. There was enough satisfied malice in his eyes to make it clear that he would ride straight into the town to spread his story. It was Big Jim who must have held him back. But why should Big Jim, who of all men in the world had the greatest reason to hate him, have restrained Buck?

Perhaps it was because the girl must appear in the story. Yet this was a motive of such delicacy that the doctor gasped as it entered his mind. It knocked down his old ideas of Big Jim. It pushed out the walls of his imagination, so to speak, and enabled him to look around the corner of a new idea.

But the more reason he had to respect Big Jim, the more reason he had to feel that he must crush the big man before he could ever marry Jacqueline. He went on again, but through the haze of his thoughts came a voice which said:

"Look out, Colby, here's Doctor Aylard coming right now, not looking none too pleased. Better scatter."

The doctor turned sharply around at that name of Colby, and he saw two men standing up in the corner of the lobby. And in one frightened face he saw a distinct resemblance to Harrison Colby.

The doctor had suffered a great deal, or else he would never have struck that cowering figure, but having been tortured that day, he wished to give back some of his pain to the world. He advanced straight upon the two. "Did I hear some one say Colby?" he asked heavily.

The white-faced youth grew a sicklier color than before. He tried to speak. It was only at the third effort that he could part his lips.

"Yes," he managed to say, "my name is Colby, too."

"It's a bad name," said the doctor brutally. "It's the sort of a name that gets men hanged or shot. Take care of yourself, Colby."

And he turned on his heel and walked away. He observed two things as he went. The one was that a sensation of the most delicious pleasure filled his own breast. The other was that the faces of the men who were near were dark with disapproval. But even that sign was no warning to the doctor. For the moment he did not care. He only wanted some other victim to trample on and to wound.

225

Then a voice spoke behind him: "Doctor Aylard!"

It was such a shaken tone that the doctor did not recognize it at first. Then he remembered dimly. It was this second Colby who was speaking to him.

"Doctor Aylard!" called the voice again.

What could be the meaning of this? The doctor turned slowly around and beheld one of the strangest sights it is ever given to a man to behold: A man half dead with fear, but prepared to fight to the death.

For young Colby stood very stiffly erect, fighting with all of his might to keep his shaking hands from stealing too near to his guns.

His eyes were wide. His mouth was drawn and the lips were bloodless. But he was prepared to push home the argument. He had rallied enough, and now he was going to resent the insult which he had just suffered as a man of honor should do.

CHAPTER TWENTY-SIX

RUSTY CORRALLED

"What the devil do you want?" the doctor roared.

"I want—satisfaction," said the trembling youth. "You can't insult a Colby like you just done with me and get away with it. It can't be done, Doctor Aylard."

The doctor had a furious inclination to snatch out a gun and crush the other with a torrent of lead. But he hesitated. Shaken with fear as young Colby was, he was nevertheless quite capable of infinitely surpassing, with his own weapon, the revolver of the doctor. For still that revolver must remain unused in the holster at his thigh, a true wooden gun in every crisis.

What was he to do? He had foolishly cornered a youngster who meant business. He could not retreat. To stand his ground meant death for him. Then, in the midst of his quandary, the heavens of inspiration opened above him, and he saw a way out which would restore him to his old position with even an added air of grace. He would be doubly endeared to the townsmen after to-day, unless he were most strangely mistaken in what he could do.

"Colby," he said suddenly, "I lost my temper just now. I've had bad news to-day, and my nerves were on edge. I'm going to ask you to forgive me for insulting you in this way."

Upon the men in the lobby the words of the doctor had the effects of thunderbolts. They gasped and stared vaguely upon one another. For a hero could certainly not have condescended to such words as Aylard had just been heard to speak. As for young Colby, his whole body sagged. A look of pain and of wonder appeared in his eyes. And then came a flush of understanding.

"Certainly," said Colby. "Don't say anything more about it."

And the doctor, with a most good-humored wave of the hand as he saw that his actions were being interpreted in the way for which he had hoped, turned again and made his way across the lobby.

The faces which had been dark with disapproval but an instant before, were now shining with enthusiasm. He went back onto the veranda, but a white-headed veteran of the range frontier followed him out and wrung his hand.

"That was the finest thing that I ever see," said the old hero. "Never knowed another man though wouldn't of blowed young Colby to the devil if he'd been inside of your boots. But I tell you, Doctor Aylard, it won't do you no harm, knuckling under when you was in the wrong.

"It shows us that there's a difference between brave men and bullies, and, sir, them last are not the kind of men that we want to have around us."

This was the opinion of the town, beyond a doubt, and as the doctor sat down upon the veranda he told himself that this was indeed his lucky country. Everything that he did in it turned out well for him, and at the finish of every predicament he found himself more gloriously advanced than before. Today, having just faced a great shame and then come front to front with eminent disaster, he had escaped from both with the most consummate adroitness.

The mouth of old Buck, for some mysterious and delicate reason, had been stopped by Big Jim. And as for the adventure with young Colby, it had placed a shining crown upon the head of Aylard as being a man who was not ashamed to admit his errors even to weaker men.

He lingered only a moment on the veranda, for he wished to get away as quickly as possible so that they would talk about him to his heart's content. Ah, had he only possessed a familiar spirit which could steal back and drink up the applause as it fell from the lips of the cow-punchers.

But he stayed long enough to see a brilliant young horseman career down the street; a fellow dressed in semi-Mexican style, with a shirt of the most brilliant blue silk, a crimson silk bandanna, with silver conches down the seams of his trousers, and a saddle mounted in silver and cinched upon a dainty-limbed black horse.

"Who," said the doctor, following with the deepest admiration the slender and handsome figure of the horseman, "who is that fellow!"

"Jud Pattison," was the answer. "The first Morne or Pattison to ride into town alone inside of the past year, I guess. He looks like a chunk out of the rainbow, don't he?"

"A Pattison in town?" said the doctor. "I thought that there were men here who'd sworn to blow the Mornes and the Pattisons off the face of the earth if they ever appeared here again."

"There's plenty that are aching for a chance to get at 'em!" admitted the doctor's neighbor on the veranda. "But since Big Jim has tamed 'em down and seems to of showed 'em how to behave, we're all sort of waiting around to see how the thing will turn out. He's done such a fine piece of work so far that it looks like he might win out."

"I doubt it," said the doctor bitterly.

"Why?"

"Because there'll be a spark of a fight started one of these days, and then everything will go up in smoke."

"If a Morne or a Pattison pull a gun," said

the other, "we ain't going to stop until we've cleaned out the whole tribe of 'em, with Big Jim included. But that time ain't come yet, and I hope that it won't come. They say that Big Jim keeps a pretty tight rein on the whole lot of 'em!"

The doctor waited to hear no more. He withdrew from the veranda, found his horse, and started on from the town toward the ranch, slowly, because he had very much to think about.

In all things he was victorious except in those things which concerned Jacqueline. And now, to win her, his whole efforts must be bent upon the speedy ruin of the Mornes and the Pattisons, involving Jim with the rest of them.

A shadow fell across the road. He looked up from the midst of his brown study and found young Colby sitting a horse in front of him.

"Doctor," said Colby, "I didn't have no chance to tell you what I thought when we was back there in the hotel. First off I got to say that Harrison Colby is a cousin of mine, but that no other Colby feels about him as if he was any better than a snake. There ain't none of him in me.

"Next thing I want to say is that I know dog-gone well that you could of downed me. And I know that it took a pile of courage for you to apologize to me. I'm out here to thank you, doctor!"

He extended his hand. There were tears of earnestness in his eyes as he spoke. And the doctor shook hands with him. More and more he was beginning to wonder at the folly which he found everywhere in human nature.

"It's done with, Colby," he told the other. "Let's both forget that it happened, except to give us a chance to make friends of one other."

Colby flushed with delight. "There's nobody else in the whole town that thinks anything but proud of you, Doctor Aylard," he added. "I've heard 'em all talk."

"Not all," said the doctor.

For a brilliant thought had come to him on the spur of the moment.

"Who says any different?" asked Colby.

"There's young Jud Pattison for one."

"What does he say?"

"Something I can't quote."

"Eh?"

"It seems he's not much of a friend of yours."

"Pattison? I dunno, but if he's out to make trouble, he'll find that I ain't one of the breed that fears him. What does he say?"

"A very ugly thing, Colby, but since I believe that a man should know who are his friends and who are his enemies, I'll tell you.

He said that I should have killed the snake when I had the chance, and that I was probably afraid to take the chance."

There was a gasp of incredulous rage.

"He said that—about me?"

"I'm mighty sorry, Colby."

But Colby wheeled his horse away in such a fury that he even forgot to say good-by. And the doctor, staring after him, laughed softly and contentedly. For his work was ended.

An hour—a day—it did not matter how long it took, but when Colby met young Jud Pattison, guns were sure to be pulled, and when they were drawn, one of the combatants would go down—no doubt it would be Colby, for it was not likely that a Pattison, trained to guns and fighting, could be beaten by such a fellow as he.

And when that shooting affair took place, it was the end of Big Jim.

So happy was the doctor that he broke into song and continued singing most of the way out to the Stoddard Ranch. His cup of happiness he considered full. But at the ranch he found that the extra drop of sweetness had been added and was awaiting him there. For, in front of the largest barn in a small corral with an extra high fence, he saw the form of a red horse, in the evening light, twisting back and forth behind the bars, and he knew that it

233

was the famous stallion. They had captured Rusty at last and brought him in.

Now they were perched on the top rail of the corral, watching the contortions of the prisoner, as he danced about like a great captured cat. The doctor could have flung his hat in the air.

But, as he drew closer to the house, he made out one note of sorrow in that time of festival. From a corner of the garden where the wall was low, behind the house, he saw Jacqueline standing, staring steadily and sadly at the splendid form of Rusty in his new prison.

The doctor hesitated. This was the least auspicious time to present himself to her, when she had not yet recovered from the first shock of disappointment and alarm. But he could not help giving himself the exquisite pain of examining at once and to the full her whole aversion for him.

He dismounted and went straight through the side gate into the garden where she stood.

CHAPTER TWENTY-SEVEN

JACQUELINE'S ADMISSION

She was so intent in staring across the wall and toward the horse that she did not see him until he was standing beside her. Then she whirled upon him with a caught breath of fear.

"Are you so sad, Jack," he asked her, "now that the time has come at last?"

He watched her fight away her alarm and her grief gallantly. At length she was able to say: "No, not because of that. But isn't it sad to see such a horse as Rusty made a prisoner?"

"Then what would you do with him, Jack?"

"Send him free to run where he chooses and do what he would do."

"But you know what happens to wild horses, Jack?"

"Well? They lead wildly happy lives."

"And come to wildly tragic deaths. They are shot by some one whose horses they have run off, or they are frozen in some hard winter. That's really what happens. Besides," he added, with a pointed emphasis, "how wild do you think that Rusty would run if I were not trying to marry you?"

Aylard saw the color run back into her face which had been so pale before.

"He would run back to his master, perhaps. Is that what you mean?"

The doctor could have groaned. "Who else would run to Big Jim?" said the doctor boldly.

He regretted that brutally phrased speech at once, but she did not wince in the least.

"Perhaps I should," she admitted. "You see, I know that you have seen us together."

"And do you despise me?"

"I only try to understand you, Clinton."

"And you never come close to it. But will you let me explain?"

"I'd rather that we didn't talk about it."

"We must. Because I have to understand a good many things."

"Very well. I can say that I don't despise you for——"

"For spying on you—say it!"

"I don't despise you for spying on me."

The words had a different and more damning sound as she spoke them.

"It's for this reason," said the doctor slowly. "I know that you don't love me, Jack. And that knowledge maddens me.

"It drives me to do things in which I can't recognize myself. It sent me out of the house to-day and over the hills on your trail, because it seemed that you must be fleeing from me when you heard that I was coming.

"Then I saw you suddenly, coming down the valley, and riding beside Big Jim, and around you galloped Rusty. I saw what a farce it was. You gave me the capture of Rusty as a goal simply to postpone the wedding, not that you really wanted him."

He paused. She made no attempt to defend herself.

"When I saw you coming down the valley by the side of Big Jim, your head was raised, and there was such a look on your face that if you wore it when I was with you, I should go mad with joy, Jack. What could I do but creep closer? I was not trying to hear you. I was simply trying to see you better."

She nodded. "Do you want me to forgive you? I do."

"And yet." he confessed, "I'd give a year of my life to hear what you were saying to him and he to you."

"Would you pay so high?"

"Yes, yes!"

"Then suppose we make a bargain. The wedding will be postponed———"

"Not a day," he blurted out. "It takes place tomorrow. I have your word, Jack, and I mean to hold you strictly to it. I'll not give way an inch———"

He paused, almost trembling for the consequences of that speech. But she was only looking down to the ground. Her hands were folded.

"Suppose I tell you, anyway."

"God knows that I want to hear."

"He came to say good-by to me, Clinton."

"To your father's house?"

"He watched until I rode out, and then he came to me."

"Ah? Lurking around the ranch, is he?"

"And he told me that he could never see me again."

"It's time that he thought of saying that. But you, Jack?"

"I asked him to tell me why. He said that it was too dangerous now. That you were coming back again. That for his own sake he dared not come near me."

"What the devil did he mean by that?"

"That he loved me, Clinton."

"The infernal, impudent rascal!"

She lifted her head. The doctor felt as though he had been struck.

"He didn't say it in words. But I understood."

"Ah? He used some fine emphasis, then. The puppy!"

"I knew, only because I love him."

The doctor shrank from her. It was not in the books that any woman should talk like this

238

at any time. Such hard-handed frankness was more than masculine, even. It had a sort of heroic and unearthly manner which cut him to the heart. As though she were burning now with such sorrowful emotion that she did not heed lesser things such as shame.

"Jacqueline!" cried the doctor, and cursed the folly of such a cry of woe and pain. For he believed in the necessity of rising above the reach of women at all times, and particularly when speaking of love. But now he had bowed his head and allowed her to see the lash falling upon his back.

"You told him that?" said the doctor, again. "Oh, Jack, did you tell him that?"

"Not a word," said she.

"But he guessed, as you did about him!"

"Guessed? As I did of him? Ah, if I could say so! But he's a child; he guesses nothing. He talks as if I were a blessed angel. He doesn't know that I'm lower than the dirt at his feet—lower than that—lower than that."

She cried it out with a passionate self-denunciation.

"There's more goodness in him than there is in all of myself multiplied by ten."

"In a gun fighter and a man-killer? In the name of Heaven, Jack, are you demented?"

"Will you let me tell you why he had come to say good-by to me?"

"Tell me, by all means."

"Because he said that in the past he had thought that you were not really a good man—not a good enough man for me. But when he heard of what you had done to Colby, he decided that a man strong enough to do that must have a great deal of good in him—that you had manners and education and culture—ah, the tears stood in his eyes when he said it. And he could not see that his own great, open heart was worth more than manners and culture a hundredfold."

The doctor swallowed and pressed his hand against his heart. Indeed, there was a very real pain there. For the tears were running down her face, and her face was raised, and yet her eyes were fixed upon the ground, as though she wished to fill her mind only with the image of the man she loved.

"Jack, Jack," he groaned, "how you love him!"

"I worship him," she said.

She said it so quietly that the doctor, for the first time, knew what was in her. He had met it once before, when he talked to an old priest of his religion. Such emotion as this was far more powerful than steel and fire, and nothing could ever change it.

"But married to a man like that—disowned by your father, cut by your friends, how could you exist?"

"If I had not a father, nor a friend—why should I care?"

She clasped her hands behind her neck and forced down her head.

"Why do I stay here to talk about him?" she whispered to herself, and not for the ear of the doctor. "Why don't I go to him and throw myself at his feet and beg him to take me?"

The doctor was shaking like a leaf.

"No," she added, "there is always my promise to my mother, and Jim himself says that promises are sacred—sacred—he says it——"

She began to sob, not a shrill, high wail such as that of most women when they weep, but a close and stifled sound, as of men who break down under a great agony. The doctor moistened his white lips. He had thought that she was a mere child. And now he felt that he had been watching the sweep of a wind across an ocean. She dwarfed him.

"Jacqueline," he tried to tell her, "after we are married, I shall find ways to make you happy—I shall find ways to do——"

She had pressed one hand across her face. The other hand she raised. And the force of it pressed the doctor back from the garden, blundering, weak-kneed, forced him through the gate, and left him gasping and weak, lean-

241

ing one hand against the outer side of the wall.

She would never respect him, after their marriage. That was very plain. For how could she respect a man who married her in spite of such a statement as she had made? But, after all, it was not respect that he wanted. It was Jacqueline, and she alone.

The very picture she made in her last grief melted into his mind with the dim beauty of a figure in an old window of stained glass.

"Big Jim has to die," he found himself saying over and over again. "Big Jim has to die — at once — at once."

That very night she might fling herself from the house, take a horse, and flee to Morne Hollow. She had the courage. She had all the will for such a wild act. And the thought made cold perspiration pour out on his face.

CHAPTER TWENTY-EIGHT

THE YOUNGER COLBY

Doctor Aylard passed Joe, the negro groom. "Joe," he called, "a horse for me — quick. The best and the fastest — the strongest that we have——"

"Yes, sir," drawled Joe. "That might be old Sammy hoss, or else might be that you'd like to take the mare from the Tomlinson place——"

"Darn your black soul, get me a horse. Move, or I'll take a spur to you."

"Yes, sir! Yes, sir!" murmured Joe, and vanished in the direction of the corrals.

But when he was out of sight he slowed down to his usual shambling walk and tugged discontentedly at the visor of his cap.

"Black skin, not soul, Mister Aylard," he added to himself. "Black skin, not soul."

As he saddled the huge black animal which was called Sam, a horse with the strength of a demon and a temper worthy of the same owner, he grumbled: "Times is going to change—oh, times is going to change!"

He had hardly finished the saddling when the doctor appeared to snatch the reins out of his hand and leap to the back of Sam. The big gelding leaped forward; the doctor flung back in the saddle. All of his might and weight lurched against the reins, and Sam's chin was jerked against his breast. The great gelding staggered and shrank against the side of the barn with a force that made it shiver. Joe, from the side, beheld with mouth agape.

"Now, damn you!" thundered the doctor.

And he gathered the big animal in hands as one gathers a little polo pony, well broken to his work. He put Sam across the corral like a streak and jumped the great gate.

"All devil! All devil in that man to-night," breathed Joe.

Down the road past the house went the doctor. He must reach Big Jim and kill him. That was all he knew in his frenzy of terror. Another horseman streaked past him as he flew away. The horseman's voice shrieked after him.

"Doctor Aylard! Doctor Aylard! Is that you?"

The doctor looked around without reining.

"Come back! Come back! The Mornes have busted loose."

The doctor let Sam run another hundred yards before he checked him. The words of the other rider had dinted into his brain by that time. He drew rein at last, however.

If the Mornes were rising there was news which would effect Big Jim. By the time he had stopped his horse an excited cow-puncher was beside him. The horse which he rode was staggering and gasping, so fiercely had it been ridden from the town.

"They're going down to Morne Hollow," said the messenger, "and they want you with 'em, doctor. You handled Big Jim once before. There ain't nobody but you that can handle him again. They sure want you bad, doctor."

"Why are they going down to Morne Hollow?" asked the doctor.

"Young Colby is shot, and Jud Pattison done it. Pattison done that dirty trick and got out of town back to the hollow. But the town is up now. They're all through with waiting for the law to handle these here cases. What we want is justice and peace, and there ain't going to be no peace so long as the Mornes are living there in the hollow."

"I thought that folks trusted in Big Jim to keep 'em all calm," said the doctor.

"We trusted Big Jim, like a lot of fools. We might of knowed that even Jim couldn't keep 'em down. Bad blood will out."

"Just how did it happen?"

"Nobody seen it all. What we piece out seems to be that Pattison was around town passing some pretty downright bad remarks about Colby. So Colby come up and asked Jud what was the straight of it. Jud didn't give him no reply except to cuss him, and when Jud had got through cussing, he reached for a gun and shot Colby before Colby could touch the handles of his Colt. That was how it was. Just plain murder."

"Murder?" said the doctor, and he could

have laughed in his exultation. "Colby died, then?"

For if Colby was dead it meant that the world would never know who first told Colby the lie about young Jud Pattison, and thereby the tracks of the doctor and his fine hand in the matter would be completely covered over. His first joy, however, did not last long.

"Not dead. But maybe dying," said the puncher.

"Maybe I can get to town to pull him through," said the doctor.

"Old Doc Maynard is handling him."

Aylard bit his lip. A black thought which had passed through his mind was banished again, as hopeless. There could only be a hope that Colby, if living, would not talk. Or that if he talked he would not count too much on the use of the doctor's name.

They rode on into the town together, and there Aylard found men gathering in the dusk for the bitter business which lay before them.

Their manner of going about it was most interesting, most surprising to him. He expected torrents of oaths, violent declarations, women whose relatives had been destroyed by the Mornes going here and there, stirring up wrath. But instead, he found a crowd as orderly as though they were merely starting out for a dance.

The only distinguishing feature was the silence in which this mob came together. For when more than half a dozen assemble, there is usually an uproar, but these people rarely spoke. On every face, however, as the doctor passed, there was a smile of welcome, and each man raised his hand.

"Good work, Charlie!" they called to the cow-puncher who had brought to them their trump card.

They were not only quiet and grim, but it seemed to Aylard that they were even a little disgusted with the prospect which lay before them.

"They don't seem very happy," he suggested to Charlie as they reached the hotel.

"They ain't," answered Charlie. "Nobody likes to go out, ten to one, and murder a lot of gents. But we've stood the Mornes around these parts for twenty years, and we can't stand 'em no longer. The time was when they didn't have nothing. They were just beggars, too lazy to work, too mean to do nothing but fight and steal.

"But then along comes Big Jim. He's got the power to make 'em settle down and work, somehow, God knows how. He cleans up the swamp. He gives them the richest piece of farm land in the whole range, where they can all live fat and easy without doing enough work to raise a sweat ten times a year. He fixes 'em up on speaking terms with a bank for the first time in the history of the Mornes. He's got everything smoothed out for 'em.

"Finally he picks out a gent among 'em that he thinks will keep the law. He sends on young Jud Pattison. The first time that anybody comes to town from Morne Hollow in years. But did anybody lift a hand agin' him? Nix! We all stood by and watched and waited to see if Big Jim hadn't maybe done a bigger work than we even imagined. And dog-gone me if it didn't seem like he'd succeeded. He'd whipped 'em all into shape, it looked like, for here was young Jud Pattison riding around town bright and cheerful and acting proud as a peacock, but not a bit sassy. He was dressed up like a party, but that wasn't nothing agin' him. I used to dress pretty flashy myself, when I was a kid. Speaking personal, it does me good to see Pattison. He looked clean, he rode clean, his hoss was a picture that was pretty good to see.

"But then came the smash. He shoots up young Colby and that busts the bubble. We see that even when they got fixed with money, still the Mornes ain't any good. They're just nacheral murderers and throat cutters. And that's why we're going to wipe 'em out. When we get through, there ain't going to be a one of

248

'em that'll be no trouble to the folks around these parts. And we're going to begin with Jud Pattison."

"What about Big Jim?"

"Nobody'll hunt trouble with him."

"What!" cried the doctor.

"You talk up almost as though you'd like to see him smashed with the rest. But ain't we seen Big Jim fighting hard to keep the Mornes straight and almost winning out?"

He added: "But when we come to get the others, Big Jim can't be kept from fighting and fighting hard and fast. And that's how he'll go down."

The doctor breathed more easily. They had dismounted now, and they climbed up the steps and into the hotel. There they found young Colby, lying in the center of the floor of the lobby, just where he had been put down on a mattress, when he was first carried in after the shooting.

And a gray-headed man, rising from his knees beside the wounded man was saying: "He'll come through all of this fit as a fiddle. Don't worry about him any more!"

Doctor Aylard bent his handsome head above young Colby.

"Well, Colby?" he asked.

He heard the answer: "I'm coming through, Doctor Aylard."

Aylard attempted to smile, and was only moderately successful.

"But I'm glad you told me what he said," said Colby. "I don't hold it agin' you none that you carried that tale to me!"

There was the story out of the bag. The doctor set his teeth. The only hope he had of covering the lie from detection was that young Jud Pattison would be killed before he was captured. The matter looked darker and darker for him.

"Very well, Colby," he said. "We'll have Pattison for this!"

"I don't want them neither. What I want is a talk with him. Because I don't see what he could of had agin' me to make him say what he did say about me. There wasn't no reason. That's why I want to see him."

"After he tricked you and shot you down?" asked Aylard.

"He didn't trick me, really," said Colby. "He was just fast as a flash getting out his gun. That was all fair enough. I got no call agin' him for that."

There was a murmur of surprise among the bystanders.

"Here," said Aylard with a growl, "let's get out of this and start for our work before morning comes. Colby is raving. Ever hear of a man getting beaten so badly in a drew that he was shot fairly before he could pull his gun half-way from the holster?"

There was a muttering agreement, but young Colby was still protesting as they filed out from the lobby and gathered in the street. Then began a squeaking of saddles and saddle leathers as men mounted. And when they had assembled, some one called out: "Who gives the orders?"

Almost at once three or four voices called: "Aylard is the man for us."

There was a cheer, and at the thought of his immense popularity, so vividly proved here, the doctor drew in a breath as though he were drinking the sweetest wines.

But he must not be associated with this expedition as the leader. There might be legal inquiries afterward. Above all, he must not appear in the eyes of Jacqueline as the instigator of the business.

He reined Sam to the side until a shaft of light fell across him. Then he raised a hand and secured silence. Sitting picturesquely in this fashion, he thanked them for their confidence, but suggested that he did not know the country as well as some others who were present. Besides, it would be better that an older and wiser head should take a hand in these affairs.

He was applauded for his speech. There was nothing he could do and say, so it seemed, that would not bring forth applause. In this town he was like a king.

"Name a man!" they called to him.

He hesitated not an instant, but named Sim Harper, the veteran blacksmith.

Sim accepted the office with sufficient gravity.

He made a speech in which he stated that this was a sad business and a bad business, but that since it had to be done, they were going to do it properly.

They answered with cheers. They called for orders. He gave them simply and clearly. He named ten men to sweep in a long loose line in advance of the main body and stretch across the top of Morne Valley, in case the clan strove to retreat before the posse arrived. With the rest, Sim Harper pushed straightforward for Morne Hollow.

CHAPTER TWENTY-NINE

JUD'S RETURN

Had Jud Pattison been just a shade older, he would not have dreamed of leaving the town to return to Morne Hollow.

He would have cut away cross country and

found a refuge in the higher mountains, and having taken this step, he would have classed himself forever among the criminals who cannot be changed or reformed. Indeed, as Jud rode back toward the hollow, he cast more than one glance at the upper mountaintops; they had their attraction for him.

Half of his heart yearned to be among them in the wilderness, hunting his food, cooking it at a cautious camp fire of his own building, keeping on the alert against the world, striking when he was least expected, and vanishing away when he was struck at in turn.

There was enough of the panther in his make-up to plant an impulse toward all of these things. But there was also in him something just a shade stronger than instinct, and this was the command of Big Jim.

When he sent Jud forth as his emissary to the town, to represent the Mornes and the Pattisons, his last caution had been: "If anything goes wrong, and if you make any slip, no matter what, come straight back here to the hollow and·tell me about it. Understand?"

And he had spoken with a cautioning, raised forefinger, the forefinger of the left hand and not of the right.

Jud often wondered why the chief used that left hand for everything. When he sat at table, he was rarely seen to lift his right hand from his lap. He ate with the left. He gestured with the left. When the younger Mornes and Pattisons asked him why, he shrugged his shoulders and told them to go about their business.

So they went to John Morne, who was supposed to know everything worth knowing, in Morne Hollow. And he told them, with a grin and a twitch of the eyebrows, that there was usually one good reason for it when men preferred to eat with the left hand. It was because the right was thus habitually kept in reserve for important action should the need arise.

This explanation was accepted, and thereafter the youngsters looked upon Big Jim with more concern and awe than ever before. It was taken for granted that John Morne must be right, and that Big Jim kept his right hand in his lap to have it ready for the use of a revolver if a crisis came.

"Come straight back to the hollow," Big Jim had said. And accordingly, straight back to the hollow rode Jud Pattison, as though a hypnotic influence were drawing him. It was in vain that he told himself he was riding into a trap and that the sheriff would hunt for him first in the big lair. He could not persuade himself to hold away, nevertheless, but he went straight forward to the hollow.

First he unsaddled his horse and turned it into the corral. Then, from his own string, he picked out the most durable mount, roped and saddled it, and tethered it under a tree before the house of John Morne and Jim Conover. When his retreat was thus prepared, he knocked at the door of the house, and then threw it open.

The harsh voice of Big Jim struck him suddenly in the face. "Since when have you started walking into my house before you're asked in, Pattison?"

Jud stepped back until his shoulders flattened against the wall. He peered into the bright haze of light which flooded out from the lamp on the center table. Big Jim was behind that light haze. Sitting in his chair he seemed more gigantic than ever. The furious retort which had risen to the lips of Jud Pattison was choked away.

Presently he began to turn his sombrero in his hands, nervously. It began to be harder and harder to keep his eyes fixed upon the face which was behind the light mist. And at last he looked down to the floor. Some one stirred in the farther corner, and, without looking up, he knew for the first time that old John Morne was there and had witnessed his humiliation.

Big Jim spoke again, and his voice changed. For it was known throughout the hollow that submission changed him marvelously.

"I was a little rough on you then, Jud. But I see that you've been into mischief. Well, so have I, in my time. It's nothing new for a Pattison or a Morne to come home to the hollow with bad news. How bad is this news that you're bringing us?"

Jud, at this, forced his head up, but still he was sick at heart. It began to appear a greater and greater crime, this thing which he had done when he was dispatched to the town as the very emissary and herald who was to proclaim to the world the peaceful intentions of the clan of Morne.

"I see what it is," said Big Jim again. "You don't have to fear me, Jud. Now that the mischief is done, I'll be found standing by you through thick and thin."

He went on: "Tell me just how it happened."

"I'm shamed," murmured Jud.

"Come, come, Jud. Some one laughed when you rode by him, and you knocked him down with that straight left I've taught you to use."

Once more the head of Jud sank, and now Big Jim dragged himself up from his chair and came slowly across the room. In the excitement of that instant, he forgot his usually well-taken precautions, and now he allowed his right foot to lag and to drag noisily across the floor. But Jud himself was too filled with fear to see smaller details.

"In the name of Heaven," groaned the giant, "what *did* you do, Jud?"

"I couldn't help it," gasped out Jud. "I swear that I couldn't, because when he came up to me, cussing and raving like a madman——"

"Who?"

"Young Colby."

"What's he got agin' you?"

"Never knew he had a thing agin' me, till he started in saying that I was a swine for calling him a coward."

"Did you ever say that about him?"

"Never hardly knowed him before. For what he done agin' Doctor Aylard, why I think that was pretty fine, just the way that everybody else thinks, too."

"Did you explain that there was a mistake, and that you'd said nothing against him, Jud?"

"I tried to say it, Big Jim. On my word of honor, I sure tried my level best to say it. But dog-gone me if I could. I jest simply couldn't bring myself around to making any explanation to him. He seemed to be so aching for a fight that—that I thought it would be a foolish idea not to give him what he wanted."

"So you——"

"Big Jim, I'd give half the world if I could undo it ag'in!"

"Jud, you shot him!"

There was a gasp from old John Morne.

"I shot him," murmured Jud wretchedly.

"He's dead?" snapped out Big Jim.

"I dunno. I guess so. Maybe not."

He added fearfully: "I'll go back and meet 'em when they come. I'll let 'em take it out on me. There ain't any sense in having all of the boys pay for what I done—only, you told me to come back to the hollow, Big Jim, no matter what happened."

"We'll never give you up, lad," cried John Morne, who could repress his spirits no longer at such a time. "I'll see every one of us damned sooner than I'll see you taken away from us."

But Big Jim had now come close to Jud and commanded. "I'll run this little show, and now that Jud has spilled the beans all over the place, I dunno but that I *shall* give him up!"

Jud shrank back to the door, and laid his hand upon the latch.

Big Jim had begun to walk up and down the room, thoughtfully, and still dragging the right foot as he strode. But the movement of Jud did not escape him.

"If you try to sneak away," he said, "I'll kill you with my own gun and give you back to the sheriff. You can write that down in red and believe it."

He said no more for the moment. But Jud, during a long second or two, glared at the giant's profile, and then at the dragging right leg.

There was no doubt in his mind, now, that this was a permanent injury. It explained the inaction of the right hand at the table. It explained many a thing, and Jud was half tempted to take the chance and leap for the door again and so out into the night. Particularly, when no revolver was strapped over the thigh of the big man.

Yet he was not able to move. For there were limitless possibilities in this man. He was capable of everything and anything. He had failed in only one fight in all his life, and his failure in that case must have been due to the purest bad luck.

In the meantime, he had worked a little miracle in Morne Hollow. He had dragged them from penury to easy life in the space of a few weeks. He had toughened their arms and strengthened their shoulders by the work on the farm. And the realest miracle in the eyes of all of them was that he had actually been able, in some way or other, to keep them to their tasks.

No, decided Jud Pattison, this was not a

man to be undertaken carelessly in a fight.

"Is this any time for talking and palavering?" roared old John Morne. "They'll be on us any minute, the damned bullies and murderers."

"There's time enough," replied Big Jim calmly. "I know them. And I know that they're still enough afraid of me to organize before they come to arrest a Morne or a Pattison here in the hollow."

He said it in such a way and with such a resolute shake of the head that the older man caught a glimpse of a monster of pride in Jim.

"D'you think that a whole crowd will stop to think about what you might do to 'em?"

"That whole crowd will stop to think about it," said Big Jim." "You can lay to that."

And he went on walking.

"But, Jim," cried the old man, "what is there to take time over? We know that the whole town will be turned out agin' us. We know that the whole lot will ride out here to murder us. There ain't more than one first step for us. And that is to get the boys under arms. After that we can figure out whether it's better to fight right here or else go back into the mountains——"

"The mountains!" shouted Jud joyously.

"Quick!" called old Marne.

"Stay where you are," said Big Jim. "I'm

handling this here game. I'll do the commanding. I'll do the talking, too."

The other two stared at one another, the youth at the old man in the wild hope and fear that a word from John Morne might justify an act of revolt and rebellion. And the old man stared at Jud Pattison, hungry to speak the needed word, and yet holding back because of something which he could not explain.

For still in that ruined body of Big Jim, which stalked back and forth through the room, dragging the right foot, there was a suggestion of mysterious power, and the miracle was ever present to them.

Through all of these weeks he had kept them from committing one overt act of violence. And in the short space of these weeks he had given them an assured and comfortable home.

But what could he do in the face of the danger which must be reaching rapidly toward them on the road from the town? Yes, even now it seemed that they heard the roar of hoofbeats. And if they could hear the horses galloping, it meant that the riders were close indeed, for the wind was blowing stiff and steady from Morne Hollow toward the town.

CHAPTER THIRTY

"A SQUARE TRIAL"

It was Jud who heard it first and ran into the middle of the room. His gesture brought John Morne to his feet.

"They're coming," cried the old man. "They're coming, Jim! Let's give the word now to the boys to arm——"

"You talk like a fool," said Big Jim Harshly. "Haven't you ears as good as the ears of any man? I don't hear nothing, and there's nothing to hear. Listen ag'in." And he raised his hand.

In fact, either they had been deceived before or else a strengthening of the wind had washed away the current of noise which they had seemed to hear.

"There's plenty of time," continued Big Jim loudly. "When I give the signal we can have every man jack with us in a couple of minutes, but in the meantime I have a plan in my head how——"

But now the roar of hoofs swept clearly into the valley. There could be no mistaking. It increased as suddenly as the noise of a band which turns a corner into the street where one is standing. It meant that scores of horses, literally, were pounding down over the brim of Morne Hollow, and were about to charge among the houses.

On the backs of those horses sat experienced fighters, and they had come to put an end to the reign of the Mornes in the valley. All of this was suddenly made clear by the rushing sound of the hoofs.

"They're here," cried John Morne, wringing his hands. "They're here. Jim, did they buy you to betray us? Jud, get the horn and blow——"

But as Jud started for it, he was caught by the shoulder and jerked back with such force that he staggered the entire length of the room before he brought up against the wall. Big Jim, in the meantime, had taken the horn from its hook, but it was not to blow the warning note upon it. Instead, he cast the horn into the open fire where the flames immediately curled around it. The call to the Mornes would never be blown again in the old note!

"Jim, Jim," cried Jim Morne, "are you giving us up?"

"What good would the signal do now?" said Big Jim. "It would only send the boys out of their houses to be caught and murdered in the open. Isn't that plain?"

Plain it was, now. Ten seconds before it might not have been so true, for the whole clan was taught to answer that call with all the speed of which they were capable. But the onrush of the riders had now brought them up to the outskirts of the houses and then carried them with a sudden yelling through the center of the hollow.

That outburst of Indian screaming so curdled the blood of John Morne and Jud that they were incapable of moving, but Big Jim had hurried to the rack at the side of the room where the rifles lay, a round half dozen of murderous repeaters. With such weapons the three of them, crippled though two were, could wash every door and window opening into the room with torrents of lead.

"Give me one!" cried Jud, and sprang forward.

He was waved back.

"Shoot him down—take one—he's sold us!" screamed John Morne.

"What's the idea, Jim?" pleaded young Pattison.

"The idea is that you go back with them."

It stunned both of the others, and still they did not seem to believe. Then a voice began to call outside the house: "Morne, John Morne! Oh, John Morne!"

And John Morne thrust out his jaw.

"It's the blacksmith come for me at last," he replied snarlingly. "I gave him a thrashing once, years back, and he swore then that he'd hang me from my own rafters. Now he's come to do it!"

The voice of the blacksmith changed its cry: "Big Jim!"

Jim walked to the door of the house and wrenched it open; instantly a rifle cracked, and a bullet sang through the opening and hummed past his head.

If he had winced to one side a volley would have followed, and then a universal rush against the houses in the hollow. For by this time every house was surrounded, and from the confused sounds in all the houses except that of John Morne, and by the absence of lights, it seemed that they had indeed taken the hollow by surprise. Yet this seemed impossible.

"Well?" called Big Jim. "Did you call me to my door to murder me?"

He looked at them grimly.

"No more firing till I give the word," sang out the nasal tone of the blacksmith. "I'm running this here little party right now. And while I'm running it I'm going to be obeyed. You—all hear me?"

There was a rattling response of single voices. It told the prisoners how immense

265

were the odds against them. But every one spoke encouragement for the smith and shame upon the anxious marksman.

There was one exception to the rule, however, and this was Doctor Aylard. He was bitterly regretting, now, that he had not accepted the leadership of the party. For if it had been in his hands he would have launched their whole power at once against the house, and its defenders, and so have hewn down Big Jim.

To the man nearest him he muttered: "The best way for every Morne to be is dead. Am I wrong, partner?"

"Right, doctor," said the youngster, proud of being appealed to by so eminent a man.

"Well," said Aylard, "we'll let 'em talk a little while, at least, and see what's what."

And he strained his eyes to make out, through the leaves of the tree which screened him, the form of the big man who stood in the doorway. This was increasingly possible, for in the room behind Big Jim there was a play firelight, and against it his body was in relief.

"Jim, is he here?" asked the blacksmith.

"Is who here?"

"You know who I mean. Jud Pattison."

"What if he is?"

"We want him and we're going to have him. Understand?"

"To use him for what?"

The answer was first of all a savage roar, and then the single voice of the leader, saying: "To use him as we see fit to use him."

"Does that mean the hanging of him to the next tree?"

"Maybe it does. It ain't for you to ask."

"Why not?"

"Because if you don't send him out to us, we're coming to take him. And if we come to take him, he ain't going to be all that we go away with."

Again the beast—for what other name does a mob deserve—grumbled furiously among the trees.

"How is young Colby?"

"That ain't your business. Pattison done his best to murder him. That's all that we're interested in."

"Didn't he fight fair?"

"Whether he fought fair or not ain't the point. What you darn well know is that a Pattison dared to pull a gun inside the town, and it's going to be for the last time, Big Jim."

Here a number of voices broke in.

"You state everything fair and square," they told their leader. "But we're getting cramped waiting for all this talk to be finished. We want action—action!"

"You'll get it, too," said the leader. "What do you say to me, Jim?"

"I say that this here is all about a mistake. In your town you got some dirty skunk who's trying to make trouble for the Mornes. He told Colby that Jud had insulted him; Colby come raving and cussing to Jud. There was a draw of guns, and Colby come out second best. Ain't that the true way of telling the story?"

"There's always been a way for a smooth talker like you, Jim, to explain away everything, but it ain't going to be enough just now. It ain't going to last at all! What we want is Jud Pattison. I got a watch here in my hand, and if the minute runs out that's starting now before we have Jud—then Heaven help every one of you that hang out in the hollow. We'll have you all!"

Some deadly portion of the minute passed with dragging seconds, and it could be seen that the big form in the doorway swayed.

At length Jim called: "Jud is just a kid. He's made his mistakes before, and this will be his last one. What you mostly want is to get me. Boys, you can have me. I'll make a fair exchange. I step out from this here door and you're free to finish me anyways that you want to. Look here!"

A gasp of amazement ran through the circle. It sounded like a sighing of the wind.

"Will you hear it? Do you hear it?" stammered the boy who was nearest to Doctor Aylard.

"A sham!" said the doctor.

For he was furious as he saw Big Jim approach his death scene with a dignity which would break the heart of Jacqueline when she heard, and make her true to him forever.

"But look," breathed the boy.

"Here's my guns and my cartridge belt left behind," went on Big Jim.

They dropped with a clang and a flop of the straps. He took a pace forward and added: "There's my knife with the rest of it. I've got no sign of a gun on me. There ain't no way that I can defend myself. Boys, you're welcome to me. I've done what deserves hanging, most like, but let the kid go free, and let the rest of 'em go, too. Things are just starting to look up around here and—"

The wonder of the spectators broke out in something like a moan.

"Go back, Jim," called the blacksmith, so moved by his astonishing proposal that his voice shook.

The quivering voice of the smith was like a key which unlocked unsuspected gentleness in the bosoms of the riders who lay in wait. There was that faint gasp again, but this time it was almost a sob.

"God knows that I believe you're fair and

269

square. Jim, for my part," said the smith. "Walk right on out from that there house and come to me where I'm standing now and I'll guarantee that you won't be touched. You've proved yourself to be something more'n a gun fighter. We like you fine. Jim, step out here to me and shake hands."

"Will he do it? Will he do it?" whispered the voice of the boy beside Doctor Aylard.

"You young fool, be quiet," groaned the doctor, and he gripped his weapon. Here he had lost his golden chance; Big Jim would live unmolested, and the calamity which he had set in motion would plunge down like an avalanche and sweep away all except the one tree which he wished to uproot!

"Thanks," said Big Jim. "That's mighty white, but it seems as how a man can't leave his kind when they get in a pinch. I stay here if I have to."

"Listen to him!" whispered the boy beside the doctor. "Ain't he about a thousand per cent man?"

But as for the doctor, his relief was not altogether unmixed with a shadow. For he was seeing the truth about Big Jim for the first time; he was looking through and through the man's heart, and he was finding there enough goodness and strength to fully explain why Jacqueline loved him.

Indeed, it was only the bullet from the doctor's gun which had given those qualities an opportunity to develop; it was that bullet which made Jacqueline love his rival. And the irony of it made him half sick and half enraged.

"I make one more proposition to you, boys," said Big Jim, as the minute verged upon the last fatal seconds. "I'll make Jud come right out here to face you. He ain't afraid to take the blame for what he done. He don't want to drag everybody in the hollow into the mess. But he thinks that you ain't going to give him a fair trial. Boys, will you give him a fair trial right here?"

"To the devil with the trial. Action!" shouted Doctor Aylard, who saw his secret coming perilously close to the light.

"Action!" called a score of other voices.

But the bull throat of the blacksmith drowned out the others.

"Hear me sing, boys! Big Jim has talked like a man, and he's going to be heard. No matter what we do with Jud and the rest of 'em in Morne Hollow, it ain't going to do no harm to hear Jud speak up. What's the prize?"

"The prize is," said Big Jim, "shall you hang Jud Pattison here and now, or does he go to jail and get his regular trial and the help of a lawyer, and all such."

271

The novelty of such a "legalized" lynching party appealed instantly and powerfully to every one, so it seemed, except to a few fierce natures who wanted to see the butchery commence at once. And among them was Doctor Aylard. Every moment of delay meant that the passions of the vigilantes were cooling. The whole raid promised to be nothing but a "dud" after all.

"Boys," he called, "are you going to be talked out of what you came here for?"

"Thanks, Doctor Aylard!" called Big Jim. "It ain't hard to see that you have been building up a taste for blood lately. I'm glad to see your hand!"

"You infernal rascal!" thundered the doctor.

But a rising murmur made him stop. It was plain that his attitude was not popular. He ground his teeth and waited.

"Step out, then, both of you," said the blacksmith.

"We'll give Jud a square trial. And he hangs or goes to jail."

CHAPTER THIRTY-ONE

JUDGE AND JURY

In the first place it was by no means certain that Jud Pattison would trust his life to the wolves. When Big Jim stepped back into the doorway he found old Morne busily persuading the youngster not to take such a desperate chance, with Jud half or more than half inclined to follow the advice. As for Big Jim, old Morne straightway denounced him. He was either a traitor or a fool, or both.

"But," said Jud, "it's a queer sort of a traitor that offers to exchange his life for your life. You got to admit that, I guess." And he turned to Jim.

"It's this way," said the latter. "If you come out here and stand your trial fair and square, you got a chance of winning out."

"One chance in ten!" cried John Morne scornfully.

"About one in ten," agreed Jim gravely. "But the other way, there's no chance at all. If you *don't* go out there and take that chance, it means that before morning there ain't going to be anything but women and children living in the hollow. It's for the sake of the others more than your own sake!"

That appeal was not wasted. Jud made his preparations slowly, as though he hoped against hope that old John Morne might find a more striking argument against going out for the trial. But though old Morne made quantities of noise, he made very little sense, and eventually Jud Pattison walked out through the door at the side of Big Jim, and both of them were utterly disarmed.

They confronted a new scene. The riders had drawn forth from the shadow. Half a dozen had collected quantities of firewood from the nearest woodshed. With bark and papers and dead twigs they made the beginning while Big Jim was in the hut persuading his companion to accept the risk.

Then, as the flames burst up, they placed on the wood, and the fire burned yellow, then red, then raised a tall and nodding head of flame. It illumined the other houses of the Mornes and showed the faces crowding to the windows, and it shone fiercely back from the glass. Nearer at hand, however, it marked in red light and in black shadow the faces of the men who were circled about it, ready to be at once judge and jury over a man whose condemnation they had already voted in their hearts.

But that was not all. Hardly a man in that outfit but had borne, at one time or another, a cross which was made for him by the men from the hollow.

There were some whose brothers had fallen under the guns of the reckless riders. There were some who had lost only distant relatives. There were some who had suffered insult and indignity in public places; there were some who had gone in dread of death at the hands of the ruffians for years. Many had been plundered in cattle raids by the expert thieves who dwelt in the hollow, and every man now turned upon Jud and his companion gloomy scowls.

The very youth and good looks of the former now told against him. He was very young, indeed, but even so early he had showed that he was capable of playing the part of a man.

He carried himself as undauntedly in the face of this peril as though he were sauntering out to greet old and dear friends of his; and the set jaw, the full and flashing eye, the high-headed indifference were all marks placed savagely against him in the reckoning. He was almost lost before his trial began.

"He's only a kid," some one remarked. "He ain't more'n a pup."

"That ain't what you'd say if he sunk his teeth into you!" rejoined his partner in the conversation, and this was the remark which raised the laugh.

It was a short laugh, swallowed almost sooner than it was begun. For every man in the circle was realizing the marks of the wolf breed as exemplified in this young fellow. Brown and straight as an Indian he looked, and his dark eyes, they vowed to one another, were capable of cruelty. So they hardened themselves against his youth.

If he had cringed, if he had broken down and wept, all would have gone well enough. They would have freed him because he was simply little more than a child. But because the boy bore himself like a man he received a man's harsh treatment.

"I'll be the judge," said the blacksmith, "and all the rest of you has got to be the jury. With you, Mr. Aylard, for the foreman. Which, it seems to me, it would be a pretty good idea for you to ask the questions that comes into your head from time to time. And on the other side, I guess that Big Jim will do the main talking for the prisoner. Bill and Joe, yonder, you take charge of young Pattison. You got to answer for it if he gets loose."

He had chosen in the mob two brothers whose father had fallen, as rumor put it, by the gun of old John Morne himself. That they could allow one of the wolf breed to escape was ridiculous past speech.

The head of the fire now waved high and free and cast its wild light brightly over the stern faces, changing each so that his companions scarcely knew him. The blacksmith took his seat upon a thick log and cracked the butt of his heavy Colt against a rock which was before him, in lieu of a desk, perhaps.

"What's your name?" asked the judge, pointing at young Pattison.

"I guess you know," said Jud, shrugging his shoulders.

"Son," said the judge, "that's something that the law sure enough hates to do—it doesn't want to hang no man that ain't got no more than a nickname. What's your real name?"

"Judson Pattison," said the prisoner.

"Judson Pattison," said the blacksmith, "d'you know what you stand accused of here?"

"I reckon I do."

"Let's hear what it is. Nope, it ain't regular for you to tell us what you're accused of. Doctor Aylard, d'you mind stepping out and saying why for Judson Pattison is here?"

The doctor was delighted. It was his purpose to work up the indignation of the crowd to such a pitch that finally the hanging of Jud might take place, and that hanging be simply

277

the spark which set all of their passions on fire.

He strode within the inner circle, leading his horse with the reins caught in the crook of his arm. He made a new note. His careful clothes, his serene face, his one hand dropped into a pocket of his riding breeches, his other hand playing idly with his riding crop. All eyes, of one accord, glanced from the tall and graceful figure of Aylard to the no less lofty form of Big Jim.

They were the two great antagonists. The doctor had conquered once, and they believed that if a contest of skill against skill came again, he would win once more. But this was a different matter. Power of hand would not tell, but cunning of tongue would.

Here the doctor would strive to hang a prisoner, but Big Jim, on the other hand, must strive with all his might to prevent that thing. All the odds were on the side of the doctor. Yet it was a contest between two old enemies, and therefore it was worth watching. The edges of the circle pushed back, and then contracted at the sides.

There remained a straight, strongly fenced alley which led from the doctor at one end to Big Jim at the other. And upon one side stood the two guards with Jud between them, his arms bound cruelly tight behind his back.

The tone of the voice was careless, casual—a tone which takes things for granted.

"It seems to me," said he, "that his honor"—and here he indicated the blacksmith with a courteous inclination of the head— "might have chosen a better prosecuting attorney. All that I know of the Mornes and the Pattisons is very brief. No doubt there are men here who can trace back their history deed by deed. But the main truth is, I believe, that in the old days before the law came, these Mornes and Pattisons lived very much as they pleased, and what most pleased them was to live by robbery, and murder their victims to cover their traces.

"But when the law came, they were clever enough to settle down and pretend to live honestly. They had a wise old leader who taught them how to ride by night, kill by night, wash off the blood, and come back to their houses by morning with clean hands."

Here he was interrupted by a rumble of indignation.

"But when the posses rode out on the murder trails," continued the doctor, "I believe that they used to come finally to Morne Hollow, and there they found that their accusations were met by all manner of oaths. There were twenty Mornes and Pattisons ready to swear that the accused man had not left the

279

hollow for the past forty-eight hours.

"Unless the posse was very strong, it did not even dare to ride into the hollow, if it found that the trail led in that direction. And, in fact, though for all of these years Morne Hollow has been famous as a hole in the wall where criminals are produced by the score, and where robbers and murderers are sheltered from the law for a price, yet during all of this time only one man has actually been arrested in Morne Hollow. And that is this rascal—this fellow, Judson Pattison, who seems to have poison in him, young as he is. Considering his age, I may remind you that a young rattler can kill a man as well as an older one can."

The doctor ceased. The last few words had been heard, but only because he had raised his voice so that it rose above the growing mutterings of the crowd. For the words of the doctor had called into their minds a thousand wrongs which they had endured.

"Let's wipe this skunk out of our way, and before he's done kicking, we'll get after the rest of the varmints."

A dozen speakers called for such action. There was a beginning of confusion. The judge was striking upon his rock in vain and calling for silence. But it required a greater voice and a greater presence than that of the blacksmith to curb the forces which were beginning to move. That voice was heard thundering from the farther side of the circle.

"Gents, are you going to square up old killings by doing a new one? Are you going to hang this poor kid before you've heard him?"

"Hang him and he damned to Big Jim and the rest of his man-killing kind," called the doctor, in tones equally huge.

If he had been silent, perhaps the crowd would have pushed ahead with its work, and short would have been the shrift of Jud. Already not one rope, but two, had been knotted around his neck. A dozen strong-armed men had presented themselves as willing and eager to hoist his body over the arm of a tree and send his soul flying on wings.

Poor Jud was trembling from head to foot. He felt less of a man than he had been feeling before this day. He was shrinking back into the child again. And unless he kept an iron hold upon himself he knew that his lips would tremble and that the tears would rush from his eyes.

Now the crowd heard the thunder of the voices of the two big men contending together, Big Jim at the one end and Doctor Aylard at the other, and out of respect for them both, it neglected the work to which it was putting its hand, fell back, and forgot the hanging of Jud for the sake of listening to these two antagonists.

"Give Big Jim a hearing," called more than one.

"What can he have to say?"

"That's for us to find out. Shut up and listen to him!"

The scene was suddenly restored to its former order. The lines reformed. And the tapping of the blacksmith against the rock could be heard as he called them back to order.

"We've heard the doctor talk on one side, and doggone me if he didn't say the truth. Now we'll hear Big Jim, so's the hanging of Jud will look a pile more legal and right."

The frankness of the blacksmith about his intentions raised a faint laugh, and that chuckle was a vast help to Big Jim.

CHAPTER THIRTY-TWO

JUD'S DEFENSE

"Judge," said Big Jim to the blacksmith, "what did you say was the name of the defendant?"

"The devil, Jim," said the blacksmith, "there ain't no sense to that question. You

282

know that his name is Judson Pattison."

"I thought I knew that," said Big Jim, "but I wasn't quite sure, because I seen the boys coming so close to hanging him for things that was done before he was born. They talk about shootings and robbings and killings—good heavens, partners, this here kid was six-teen only last week. How long has he been old enough to do the things that the doctor accuses the Mornes of?"

It was rather a sharp blow. The judge turned upon the doctor.

"What do you say, Aylard?"

The doctor stepped a little forward, sneer-ing, as though by coming closer to Big Jim he could make the latter shrink away in fear. But after the step or so, he seemed to change his mind.

"I say that every one knows what I meant. I was talking about the whole gang of the Mor-nes and the Pattisons. They've been bad from the beginning to the end, and every one knows that a man cannot be better than the blood he comes from."

Big Jim laughed softly, while the others wondered.

"You say that in the wrong place, doctor. There are some of our best men here that have got a pile better records than their fathers had before 'em. Back in England, where they say

that the Aylards come from, most like a gent
can't get no better than his father and his
grandfather and his great-grand-father was
before him. But here in the West, a man is
what folks find him to be."

It was unquestionably a score for Big Jim.
There were men present upholding the law
whose fathers had been ruffians of the first
water. There were men present who had been
robbed, by bullet, of their fathers in their
infancy. In another community such an hered-
ity might have ruined them. But here men
were needed too greatly for questions to be
asked.

They grew up unshamed, and all that they
asked of the world was a little forgetfulness. If
the doctor did not know this, he could guess
by the air of the men around him that he had
ventured into dangerous waters, and he
hastily retraced his steps.

"Let's get back to the case of young Pattison," he said.

"Doctor Aylard," said Big Jim, "that's just
what I'm trying to do. I'm trying to see that
Jud ain't hung for things that he had no hand
in."

"It won't help you, Big Jim," said the doctor. "We all know what sort of a man your
young Pattison is. We saw poor Colby. Who
shot him down?"

284

"Who began that fight?" asked Big Jim.

"Who always begins the fight where a Morne or a Pattison is mixed up in it?" answered the doctor sneeringly.

"Let's hear Jud speak for himself," said Big Jim. "Jud, speak up. What happened?"

"Are we going to stay here all night?" thundered the doctor. "Do we have to waste our time on this worthless brat?"

"It ain't hard to see," broke in Jim, "that his life ain't much to you, but it's more to him than anything else that he owns."

It brought another faint chuckle from the crowd. And now they began to take a new interest. They still took it for granted that the affair would end in the hanging of Jud Pattison, but in the meantime it appeared that Big Jim was distinctly overmatching the doctor.

"Order here," called the blacksmith. "There's too much noise in this here courtroom. Shut up, Si Peters. You always did make more noise than sense. Doctor Aylard, it sure looks like Jim is right, and what we're doing here is to try Jud Pattison and not the whole Morne and Pattison tribe."

"Very well," said the doctor, sullen with disappointment, "do as you please."

"Talk up, Jud," said Big Jim.

It was hard for Jud to speak. His voice came quavering and thin, at first. And that uncertainty of voice seemed to open the eyes of the crowd to the fact that their prisoner was young, very young indeed.

So, with great, straining eyes fixed before him, with frequent pauses as he fought to control himself, he told forth his story of how young Colby had rushed up to him, made the accusation, and then torn out his gun. He himself, astonished, snatched out his own weapon and fired instinctively, and poor Colby dropped to the ground.

There was a considerable pause.

"Look here," said Big Jim, "was you and young Colby enemies?"

"Nope."

"Had you ever seen him before to-day?"

"I knowed his name, and that was all."

"After he dropped, did you ride away?"

"Nope, I jumped down and kneeled beside him."

Big Jim started. This was a part of the story for which even he was not prepared. But he hurried on to take advantage of it.

"Jud," he said, "it don't seem nowise likely that you'd hang around after dropping a man."

"I sure didn't want to stay," said Jud mournfully. "I knowed that I'd raised hell, and I would of give a leg to undo what I'd started on, because I knowed that this would start trouble for everybody in Morne Hollow, and you'd told me that I was to be particular careful, and that you was sending me in just to show how plumb peaceable a Pattison or a Morne could be around town."

"What has this to do with the case?" broke in the doctor.

"Excuse me, doctor," said the blacksmith, "but I'm plumb interested in what the kid is saying. Go on, Jud. We ain't quite as hard as you think, maybe."

And the doctor, glaring savagely around him, perceived that it was true. Clever Big Jim must have foreseen that they could not maintain their rage at the killing point of heat for any length of time.

"You kneeled down beside Colby," went on Big Jim. "What for?"

"I wanted to see if I'd finished him. And I hollers out to him, 'Why did you come hell bent for me like this? Who told you that I said you was yaller?'

" 'A gent that couldn't have lied,' says he to me.

" 'Who was it?' says I.

" 'Doctor Aylard,' says he."

"A lie!" thundered the doctor, and then bit his lips with vexation, which verged toward despair.

For as he listened to the narration of the

287

boy, so clear and steadily flowing that it would have been hard indeed for any one to have disbelieved a single statement that he made, it seemed to the doctor that his heart would burst with excitement. And so, when the crisis came, and when the truth was known that it was he, after all, who had sent young Colby to his destruction, or the danger of it, he could not contain himself any longer.

He had called all eyes upon himself, now. They stared and stared as though they could not see clearly enough, and the doctor wished himself a thousand miles hence if that would keep his lie from being detected.

For a single instant, in fact, he looked exactly the part of the guilty rascal that he was. His face grew blotched with purple and with pallor. His eyes blinked and twitched rapidly away from one to the other side, and he was seen to be gnawing restlessly at his lips.

"Maybe a lie—maybe a lie," said Big Jim, and his voice rang, in the guilty ear of the doctor, like the trumpet of a condemning angel. "But the time has come for us to find out just how much of a lie it all is. Maybe when we get through finding out we'll also know just why the doctor is so hot to get poor Jud hung. Maybe we'll know why he sent Colby ravin' and ragin' to fight Jud in the first place. Maybe we'll find out them things."

The doctor had listened to so much, but he could not endure more. Black rage had rushed across his eyes and obscured his calmer judgment with a mist. He scanned the body of Big Jim, and he saw that there was no gun strapped to his right side, or to his left. No, he had abandoned his weapons near the door of the Morne shack.

And the doctor thrust forward down the lane of faces until he was confronting Big Jim at arm's length.

"You rat!" he gasped out. "You rat!"

He slashed Big Jim squarely across the face. For he knew well enough that when the big man raised a hand to protect himself he would not complete the motion to strike, for a dozen guns would be out before the hand of Jim, which had once been so terrible, was as high as his shoulder, and a dozen bullets would smash the life out of Big Jim's heart and body.

So, with his supple, cutting, riding crop, he struck Big Jim across the face and then leaped back, jerking out his revolver.

It was not until he had completed that maneuver that he saw what had happened. For half a dozen hands had grappled with his gun and dragged it down, and the bullet which he fired merely plowed into the ground.

"Good heavens, Aylard," he heard them say, "Big Jim ain't got a gun—he ain't got nothing. You wouldn't kill a helpless man."

He stared beyond their heads. What had happened to Big Jim? The face of the giant showed by the firelight as white as chalk, and across it was a bright red slit. It began at his right cheek bone. It passed down and across his mouth and on to his chin. And yet Big Jim had not stirred to strike back.

"Boys," he was saying, "I guess we're seeing the insides of the doctor fast enough. He wants me to start a fight that I can't never finish. But he don't know me, and he don't know the rest of us. Things ain't done that way in this part of the country."

A wall of hostile faces confronted the doctor. He saw the same sentiment expressed on them all. Indeed, it was the simple truth. Things were not done that way in that part of the country.

For another instant he hesitated; then he turned on his heel, flung himself on the back of Sam, and dashed away through the night.

CHAPTER THIRTY-THREE

BREAKING THE LAW

The hands of the mob were tied after that. For, much as they yearned for action, what could they do after their battle passion was spent? There was nothing for it except to return home as soon as they could. And back they went, with Jud Pattison a prisoner in their midst.

However, before they gave him to the jailer that night, a dozen men had assured him of their esteem, and that they would see he did not lack support if he came to trial.

He did not even come to trial. For, in the first place, young Colby refused to swear out a complaint against the victor in their fight, and since Colby himself was now doing very well, it was considered that it would be something less than fair to hold Jud Pattison for an offense for which he had already, perhaps, paid penalty enough.

So Jud Pattison rode freely back through the town and came to Morne Hollow in the midst of acclamations. But he went first to Big Jim, even before he went to his mother. And he wrung both of Big Jim's hands and thanked him with tears on his cheeks for the saving of his life the day before.

"I've heard of gents taking bullets for a friend," said Jud, "but never before heard of a gent standing up under a hosswhip for the sake of nobody whatever!"

And he added, his voice low and hushed: "When do you go after him, Jim?"

To this remark the big man returned no reply. He merely asked in turn: "What's the news as you was coming out of town, Jud?"

"Nothing much except what happened last night. They're all talking about that, Jim, and wondering what'll happen when you meet up with Doctor Aylard. I can tell you this: That the doctor ain't any more popular than a pup, right now. And half of the folks are saying that it's sure a pity that he's married——"

It seemed that he had stabbed Big Jim with that word. For the latter jumped to his feet with a great cry.

"D'you mean to say that she's married him? That Jacqueline Stoddard has married him?"

Jud winced before such a passion. "As good as married," he said in explanation. "The doctor is rushing everything along for to-day. He's sent for the minister. They're to be married before noon at the Stoddard place."

He broke off, for Big Jim, striding back and

292

forth through the room, was groaning aloud: "That there marriage can't come off. There ain't a place for it in the world. There'd be a curse on such a marriage as that, I tell you. I thought he was a hero. He ain't no more'n a skunk. And——"

"Then you'll go for him this morning?"

"This morning!"

Jud slipped for the house. In an instant he had spread the great news.

"We thought that Big Jim would never wake up," he told his friends. "But this morning he's going to meet the doctor. He's just told me now. He's going to meet the doctor before that there marriage comes along!"

The murmur buzzed up and down the hollow, and old John Morne, for the first time in many days, came forth and sat under the old tree where Jud had so nearly looked his last on the sky the night before, and where John himself had so often given his orders and his counsels to his clan. And there, around the patriarch, they were assembled when Big Jim came forth, mounted his horse, and rode away.

"Jim!" called John Morne.

The big man reined his horse beside the crowd. And now that he was so close they could see, under the shadow of his sombrero's brim, the gloom and the care in his face.

"Where are you going, Jim?"

"I'm going to get back Rusty!"

"Is that all?"

"That's all."

"What if you find you can't get him, and—and don't come back?"

"Then what I say is for you and the rest of 'em to sit tight. Let Hughson handle the business. He'll do it and be glad to. He's square, and he knows money. Will you let him do the managing?"

"You ain't got much trust in me, Jim?" said the patriarch sadly.

"I ain't," said Jim. "D'you really expect me to?"

The other scowled, but said no more.

"Big Jim," said a young Pattison, "will you let us ride with you?"

"Not a step. And if I go down, you stay here quiet and don't try to revenge me."

With that final instruction he turned the head of his horse and rode slowly out of the hollow. Passing through the town, he encountered the sheriff.

The latter stopped him and greeted him heartily.

"What's up, Jim?" he asked.

"Nothing," said Big Jim, "but I lost a hoss a while back, and now I'm going out to get him back!"

The sheriff turned pale. "You know what that means, Jim?"

"I know that hoss is my hoss. I'm going to get him."

"That hoss was outlawed for running off bunches of ranch stock. I dunno that you could prove your claim to Rusty in a law court."

"I ain't going to a law court to prove it."

"Jim, Doctor Aylard had swore that he'll never give up the stallion unless there's a court order served on him."

"I'm mighty sorry to hear that."

"And if you set foot on the Stoddard Ranch without a court order and agin' their will, d'you know what you'll be doing?"

"Breaking the law?"

"And breaking it bad, seeing that I've warned you beforehand!"

"Sheriff, I'm thanking you for your kindness. But I'll have to get on; the time is running short. Has the minister started out yet for the ranch?"

"He has," said the sheriff.

"I'm mighty sorry to bother him," said Big Jim, "but I guess I'll have to start on ahead."

The minister was a poor man, and as strong-handed as he was poor. He was not brought in from the East. He was as natural a product of the West as the sagebrush, and as tough of limb and spirit.

When Big Jim drew alongside of the minister's mustang and requested him to stop, the minister merely shook his head.

"Don't bother me, Jim," he said; "I'm in a hurry. It doesn't pay to keep people who want to get married waiting. It mustn't be done, because, for one thing, it cuts down one's fee!" And he chuckled at his small joke.

Big Jim reached out and jerked the mustang of the minister to a halt. "Get off!" he commanded.

Such a sudden halt had caused the hat of the minister to tumble over his right eye. He rearranged that hat now and turned upon Jim Conover a glance of fire.

"What the devil," said he, "d'you mean by that?"

"I mean," said Big Jim, "that this here marriage has to wait."

"What for?"

"Me," said Big Jim.

"What's going to happen?"

"The best man is going to win," said Big Jim.

At this the minister rubbed his chin thoughtfully, and his eyes contracted and grew brighter.

"You are going to fight the doctor," he stated at last.

"I am."

"He's beat you once, Jim."

"It ain't what I hope to do—it's what I got to do that makes me keep at this here thing, you see."

"Well," said the other slowly, "if I could stop you I would. But since I can't stop you, I'm going to get off my hoss, and tell you to remember that God fights for the just."

With this, he gravely dismounted and stood in the road without a word of complaint.

"I'll remember that," said Big Jim soberly. "Will you tell me one thing, now that we're talking?"

"Anything I can—to dissuade you from this fight, Jim?"

"Tell me first what you think of Aylard. You've seen him and talked to him and you know more than the rest of us around these here parts. What sort of man is he?"

The minister kicked at a pebble, watched it roll into a nest of prickly pear, and then rubbed his chin again.

"I dunno that a man has a right to keep opinions to himself all the time," he said, "and my idea of the doctor is that he's a hound."

"Do you mean it?" asked Big Jim.

"With all my heart!"

Conover stared at the horizon for an instant

and felt the burn of the sun scorching the skin of his shoulders.

"I'm taking your hoss away so's you can't get to the ranch," he said, "and perform that marriage."

"That's a low thing to do," said the minister.

"And I'm leaving you this for your church," said Conover. And he dropped a fat wallet into the road.

"For the poor," said the minister, raising the wallet; and it never would come into his heart that he was the poorest man in his parish!

"And if you give me a prayer while I'm gone——" muttered Big Jim, and then spurred furiously away as though ashamed of what he had said.

When he looked back from the nearest rise, leading the minister's horse, he saw that the latter had not yet started to walk away. He stood in the same spot, and the heat waves made him seem an ethereal creature of blue light and mist.

CHAPTER THIRTY-FOUR

WHIPLASHED

The doctor had picked up the magazine not because he expected to find anything in it which might interest him, but because he had to have something to occupy his eye during the interim. What he found, however, sent a thrill of curiosity through him. For the very second article upon which his eye fell was upon freak cases of paralysis; and almost instantly he was running his eye through an account of a case almost exactly parallel to that of Conover.

It was well, he told himself as he read, that he had located that magazine before any other person in the house did so. It was well, above all, that he had found it before Jacqueline.

He heard a rapid step on the corridor outside. It was Stoddard himself, and the doctor pushed the magazine under the cover of a cushion just as the rancher entered. The latter was exceedingly excited and worried.

He had been reflecting upon the wedding for a long time, he told his companion, and it seemed to him, when all was said and done, that it was rather a serious thing to rush ahead and marry a girl who seemed so set against marriage as Jacqueline.

The doctor heard him, agreed with him, and then advanced the argument which he had used before—that it was almost sacrilege to wait so long after the death of Mrs. Stoddard before executing her wish.

There had never been a reply to this before, and there was no reply to-day, except that Stoddard did not verbally agree with him. He pondered with downward eyes for a time and then went hastily out of the room, as though he wished to escape from a problem which he could not solve.

Doctor Aylard, however, sat down resolutely to his magazine article once more. He had felt rather ashamed on this last day, and many qualms of conscience which would make it difficult indeed to get through to the end of the ceremonies. But no one, it seemed, was able to fathom the depths of his baseness. No one dared consider him as low as he really had fallen in driving the girl on to the marriage.

As for Jacqueline herself—that thought had hardly formed itself between his eyes and the printed page when he looked up and saw her standing in the doorway.

He rose, and in his rising, hastily slid the

magazine with its too-informing article under a cushion. Then he went forward to greet her with both his hands extended. Instead of making an answering gesture, she shook her head.

"I can't do it," she told him. "I'm willing to play my part as well as I can when there's any one near to have an eye upon us. But you mustn't ask me to keep on acting when there's no audience."

It was a whiplash to the doctor, but he bore steadily up against it. Who will not allow the eagle's wings to beat at the very moment when the trap is closing down upon it? A few more minutes of freedom and then she was his, and after the marriage, there would be ways to teach her greater amiability! He recorded this resolution at the very instant that he was smiling upon her.

"Very well," he said. "Time is what I ask for, Jack. And with time to help me, this will turn out a happy day for you, after all."

She neither thanked him nor smiled nor shrugged her shoulders, but she looked at him with a dull and hopeless eye which showed that she had already, many times, computed the suffering which lay before her.

"The first thing to do," she said, "is to find out a place to go for our—honeymoon."

She spoke the word with a shudder.

"Why should we go any place?" he asked her.

"Are you contented here?"

"Well enough," he said. "It does well enough for me. I wish to stay here, for one thing, because in coming to know your native country better, Jack, I feel that I am coming closer to you. It's like a book about you."

"How do you explain that?" she asked him.

"Its great heart, its wilderness are among the things that teach me about you, Jack."

"Hush," she said, "please!"

She waited a moment. And the doctor wondered if he could indeed be so distasteful to her that she could not even address him without a distinct effort.

"But about our staying here afterward," she assured him. "There is one thing that you seem to have forgotten."

"What is that?"

"I'm afraid that people will not care to have you near them after last night."

"Last night?" he cried, and crimsoned in spite of himself. "Who has been talking to you about last night?"

"Who? I think that the air is full of it, Clinton. Even the sticks and the stones are talking about what a man Big Jim has proved himself to be."

"A cowardly renegade," said the doctor

hotly, "or he would not have endured what he did!"

She could not speak. She turned sharply away from him and stood at the window, breathing hard.

"Jack," he pleaded, following her, "do you hate me as bitterly as this, then?"

"I mustn't talk—just now," she said. "But oh, how could you have done such a thing when you knew that he dared not lift a hand? If he had, they would have shot him down, and then gone murdering through Morne Hollow! But——"

"But what, Jack?"

"Did you really send that poor boy, Colby, to kill young Pattison or be killed by him?"

"Have they told you that, too?"

"Yes, and I haven't believed it. It's too unspeakably dastardly. If—if I *did* believe it, Doctor Aylard, not even my oath to my mother could make me marry you."

"It was all a complicated lie," said the doctor slowly. "They have been plotting to ruin me in your eyes, you see. But in spite of that—with time——"

She raised a hand to stop him. "Perhaps—perhaps," she whispered. Then she added: "I want to be alone—in this room, Doctor Aylard!"

"Well, well," he said, determined to steer

her out of it lest she should discover that fatal magazine which lay beneath the cushion. "Why, Jack, isn't it rather odd that you should choose to spend the last hour before your wedding—and that infernal minister should be here at any time—in the ugliest room in your father's house?"

"I used to spend the afternoons here with my mother," she told him. "She used to sit there in the sunlight, and sew, and I read to her." She paused. "That's why I'd like to be here alone for a little time, Clinton."

He hesitated. Had she gone to the couch to sit down, he would have brazened the thing out until he maneuvered her out of the room at any cost of esteem in her eyes. But since she sat down in a chair by the window and looked out through it with eyes made vague with tears, he suddenly determined that he must risk it. Better, at least, not to awaken any suspicions in her.

So he turned suddenly and left the room. He had hardly stepped into the hall when a servant came hurrying to call him to the telephone. It had been newly installed at great expense, running from the town to the Stoddard ranch house. Perhaps the great length of line had been poorly put up, for the voice which called to the doctor from the other end of the line was a confused roaring.

"Hello, Doctor Aylard!" he made out the voice to say at last. "This is the sheriff!"

"Hello, sheriff!" he answered.

"I've had the devil's own time trying to locate your place, doctor."

"I'm sorry. What's wrong?"

"There's trouble coming out your way."

The voice, half lost in the weird roar of the instrument, sent a chill of despair through the doctor.

"What trouble?" he asked.

"Big Jim Morne is running amuck after you, doctor."

"Then," cried the doctor, "why the devil haven't you headed him off?"

"I've got no proof that he'll do anything wrong, but I know inside of me that he means business."

"Who told you?"

"He did. He's coming after Rusty."

"He'll be damned before he gets the horse."

"That's what I've heard you say, but— there'll be big trouble and bad trouble if you try to keep him away from it."

"He wants a fight, sheriff?"

"He wants a fight. That's the long and the short of it."

"Then he'll get it. I licked him once, and I can still lick him." And the doctor slammed up the telephone receiver and reached instinctively for his revolver.

He drew it forth and held it with his finger curling on the trigger and his jaw thrusting out. He held it for a long moment before he remembered that, after all, it was only a wooden gun, so far as he was concerned. In the quick draw which was necessary against a Western gun expert, he was quite helpless and hopeless.

But, for that matter, what could be said of Big Jim? If the doctor was bound to be clumsy, the stricken right hand of Big Jim was engaged to do no more than to blunder.

And yet, the heart of the doctor refused to warm with confidence. For, if Big Jim were helpless, and knew himself to be helpless, how did he dare to ride forth against a man like the doctor, who could not be beaten with a wooden gun—who, indeed, used a wooden gun himself.

It was a great mystery. The doctor put up his gun again, gnawed at a knuckle without bringing any light upon the subject, and then strode hurriedly forth into the sunlight and looked off down the road.

CHAPTER THIRTY-FIVE

ON THE LEFT HIP

There was nothing down the road saving its own whiteness, and the doctor took a breath of relief. At least, the danger was not immediately upon him.

Here a cow-puncher galloped around the corner of the garden wall and called anxiously to him.

"We've sighted Big Jim coming down the road, Doctor Aylard. He looks like he's aiming to come to this house, too!"

The doctor started. "Have them saddle Sam for me," he said. "I'm going to meet him."

For, since his gun was wooden, indeed, there was nothing left for him to do but to rush out and strive to impress the enemy with the boldness of his attack. And yet his heart murmured, deep within him, that it would be very hard indeed to impress Big Jim.

He walked impatiently up and down, waiting for the horse. Now that he had made up his mind, he could not have the animal under him soon enough, and when it came, he decided to charge out upon Big Jim as though he were leading a cavalry regiment against the man from Morne Hollow.

It was at this point that the greatest blow of all fell. The door of the house was jerked open. He turned and saw that Jacqueline Stoddard had run out into the garden, and in her hand was an opened magazine. That was proof enough for the doctor. Her manner, the voice in which she called for him, told the story of her discovery, and when she saw him, the doctor felt that if it had been possible to convert himself into a mist, he would gladly have done so. Her angry eyes seemed to have looked to the very heart of all of his lies since he had come to the range and lived upon the ranch.

"Doctor Aylard! Doctor Aylard!" said the girl, coming close to him and pointing to the magazine. "I think I understand now why you did not wish to leave me alone in that room. Because there was dangerous company waiting for me there. Was that it? Was that it, sir?"

He gave way a little before her fury.

"Of what in the world are you talking, Jack?"

"I wish to Heaven," she said bitterly, "that you did not know. I wish that, Doctor Aylard, but I have been guessing at the truth. I have

308

been guessing at things that sicken me!"

"You're excited, Jack. And it's very wrong for people to say what's in their heads when they're overly excited. Wait until you've quieted a bit. Then we can talk this over more quietly and find out what is troubling you. But to do that at present would be a little foolish, I'm afraid. Don't you think so, Jack?"

"I think only—that I have discovered the truth!"

"Of what, then?"

"Of the manner in which you beat poor Jim Conover!"

"Ah! Do you call him by that name?"

"Here is the whole explanation, put here in this magazine by the gift of God. It tells me what Jim always refused to tell me, and that was, why his right arm and leg were so dull and clumsy in movement. Can you guess, Doctor Aylard? Can you guess why he was so crippled that even a poor hand with a gun like yourself could beat him?"

"Am I so poor?"

"Oh, you know that I have seen you at your practice. It has been a wonder to me ever since. And most of all, I have struggled through a great problem over and over again and never come to any conclusion. Why, being such a bad shot, did you dare to meet Big Jim, face to face, after hearing my father tell what a dreadful fighter he was?

"Sometimes I have thought you a brilliant madman in your courage. But now I see what the true explanation is! Your doctor's eye saw what no other eye could see. You knew, at the first glance, that he was not half of his old self, and so you attacked a helpless man, and stepped over his fallen body to this wretched fame you have made for yourself. Oh, God, how could such a creature as you be made and allowed to walk and to live in the form of a man?"

He had thought, in other days, that if the time should ever come when she should discover that unspeakable truth, he would be guarded against caring too much what she said by the fact that he had possession of her forever, but now he found that his assurance had been mustered in vain. The blow had fallen before she was made his in the eyes of the law, and unless he could quickly dissuade her from the new opinion, she was lost to him most certainly, and forever.

"Jack," he said, "I don't even guess what you're talking about. Will you tell me simply and plainly?"

She paused and crimsoned, as though the doubt as to his guilt for the first time came into her brain.

"Big Jim," she said, "is—partially paralyzed—his whole right side is affected."

"The devil!" said the doctor, and fell back a pace in the greatest apparent amazement.

"You call yourself a doctor, and yet you didn't know that?"

He set his teeth and strove to face her. "On my honor, Jacqueline."

"Swear it!" she cried.

He raised his right hand. "I swear it!" said the doctor gravely.

But though he could control his voice, his color he could not command, and the flame swept up through his cheeks and across his forehead, burningly, to the very roots of his hair, and the perspiration stood out in great drops above his eyes. He could feel the stamp of his lie and of his shame put upon him, and he had to fight from keeping his eyes above the ground.

He could not even hope that she had failed to see. For the scorn and the anger were mixed with pity in her eyes.

"But, oh," she said, "how horribly base, how unspeakably low to strike a man who could not strike back at you."

"Jacqueline!"

But she drew back from him toward the house.

"Jacqueline," he said, "if you will let me try to explain to you how——"

"How you tried to murder him when he was

311

helpless, helpless," she cried. "I never wish to see you again."

The doctor ground his teeth. "For the last time!" he called to her. "Your oath to your mother, Jack!"

"If she knew, she would bless me from Heaven for refusing to keep that oath!"

The doctor bore the weight of her glance for another instant, and then he turned and fled from the garden, flung himself upon the horse which was being held for him, and made off.

"Shall we go along—to see that there's fair play?" called a cow-puncher to him.

"Stay here and be darned!" thundered the doctor, and passed out of the alley, into the winding whiteness of the road, and at last reached the top of the first hill. There he drew rein to take thought of his position again.

From this point the men at the ranch house could still see him, clearly outlined against the sky, though he could not distinguish them. And Jacqueline, he could be sure, was down there watching him with an anxious glance. By this time, perhaps, she knew that he had ridden out to murder her lover.

And that was the one prayer left to him— that he should be able to beat down Big Jim and ride out of Jacqueline's life having failed to win her, but having at least wrecked her chance for happiness.

He thought of all this fiercely and proudly as he sat his horse against the blue evening sky. Then he saw Big Jim drift over another hilltop and float down the slope toward him, riding leisurely, it seemed.

How strange that a man bent upon an affair of death should canter along as though there were nothing in his mind but the tang of the alkali dust in the air, the blue shadows on the sand beneath the whitened cactus, and the weight of the heat on head and shoulders and gloved hands.

His nonchalance was superb.

But now the other came closer. There had been no mistaking the fact that this was Big Jim by his manner of riding from the very first instant. But now it could be seen that if his horse galloped slowly it was only because exhaustion had slowed its gait until it could barely stagger along.

And if the doctor had wondered at the leisure before, now he wandered at the haste. What was the secret at the command of Big Jim? Had the girl told Big Jim, for instance, that he was a wretched shot, after all, and had merely bluffed his way into fame after shooting down one helpless man?

Nearer and nearer Big Jim swung on the staggering horse. And then the doctor saw something which struck, like a bullet, through his heart.

The gun did not swing at the right hip of Big Jim. Instead, it hung from a blackened holster upon his left hip. His left hand, then, would draw it—his left hand which sickness had not blasted. And though perhaps less rapid than the lightning skill of the right hand, yet that left hand must move like the motion of a striking snake's head compared with the clumsy work of Aylard himself.

"She's told him!" muttered the doctor to himself, "and I'm a lost man! A lost man! He's sure to ride me down, shoot me down!"

A shout down the road. It was the great, thick voice of Big Jim calling: "Get ready, Aylard! Get ready, you dog!"

The doctor looked up to the blue of the sky, mixed thin with sunshine. Suppose that this were his last look at that same blue sky?

"Now!" cried the voice of the rider. "Pull your gun!"

The doctor could not move his hand.

"Now!" shouted Big Jim again.

The doctor saw the gleam of steel. But what he reached for was not his own weapon. Instead, he twitched the reins to the side, swung his horse around, dropped lower over the pommel, and fled for his life down the slope.

A yell of wonder came tingling from the

314

hollow, where the cow-punchers watched, and the girl among them!

But when the doctor looked back, his heart blackened and blasted with shame, he saw Big Jim sitting on the top of the hill from which Aylard had just fled, not pursuing, but waving his hat joyously to the people beneath him.

THE END